Tempting me

JAMI ROGERS

For those who came for the banter ...

TEMPTING ME
Copyright © 2025 by Jami Rogers
All rights reserved.
No part of this book may be used for AI learning or generation, reproduced or transmitted in any form or by any means, electronic or mechanical, including photocopying, recording, or by any information storage and retrieval system without the author's written permission, except for the use of brief quotations in a review.
This is a work of fiction. Names, characters, businesses, places, events, and incidents are either the products of the author's imagination or used in a fictitious manner. Any resemblance to actual persons, living or dead, or actual events is purely coincidental.
www.authorjamirogers.com
Cover design © Hang Le byhangle.com
Editor: Julie Sturgeon, CEO Editor, ceoeditor.com
Proofreading: Emma Cook, Booktastic Blonde
Character Art by CustombyErikaPlum

 Formatted with Vellum

Tempting me

JAMI ROGERS

NOTE FROM THE AUTHOR

This book takes place at the same time as Loving You, so you will see a few crossover scenes. Enjoy!

PROLOGUE

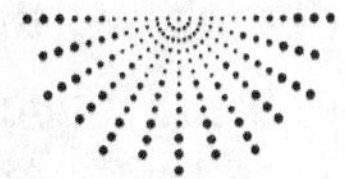

SHAY - LAST SUMMER, A.K.A. THE SUMMER OF HUDSON AND SADIE'S STORY

"Just set it down over there." I point to the left side of The Marina's front doors, where all the other construction materials have been placed, doing my best not to squeal at how excited I am right now.

It's happening.

It's *really* happening.

The Marina is finally getting the upgrade it deserves. As soon as it's done, people will return, memories will resume, and business will thrive.

Just like it did when I was a kid.

All because of me.

Yay!

Those were the best days, and I have my fingers crossed that in a few years I'll get to create those same memories with my own family.

The early summer breeze off Lovers Lake tickles my skin just enough that the eighty degree temperature of the day is bearable. There are a few people on the water, mostly those who own a boat, but we did have a few jet ski rentals today. Not as much as we used to. The bar and restaurant are outdated, and the weekend events that The Marina used to hold are nonexistent.

The Marina—yep, that's what my family named it—has been under my older brother's management for the last three years, and it's clear he doesn't see the potential I do. He let this place go, and I plan to bring it back.

First, the main building, then minor touches to the bar, then the restaurant, and finally the ten lodges we rent out. It's a long list, but I can do it. I mean, come on, the entire backside of The Marina faces the lake, with a wraparound porch that used to be *the* spot here.

One could sit and watch the sun go down just over the lake and mountains that surround it, finally hearing themselves think as the night breeze cooled the sunburn they earned after a successful day on the water. Maybe even a sweet drink in hand as their family or friends joined them for the evening, saying something like, *this is the life*.

I want that back.

Watching the company I hired unload their supplies makes me giddy with what is yet to come for this place.

"Did you have time to put a schedule together?" I ask Brent. He's my main point of contact for the company. I told him all of my goals, and he said he could get it done. I just need some proof that there is a plan. I've seen the blueprints for the final product, but I want to know their day-to-day schedule so I can have the first two parts of my plan done before snow takes over in four or five months. You really never know when it's going to hit when you live in Wyoming, so getting things done is a must.

Brent grunts, refusing to look at me, but I just keep smiling.

Hiring him and his team was already a risk because they're from out of state. When you live in a small town and there's only one option for a builder, expanding your options is just a smart business move, but people talk and I can't let this town think I made the wrong choice by hiring elsewhere.

So I choose to ignore the fact that he seems a bit sensitive that I've asked him about his plans. I don't want to chance him running off all because I can be a little … orderly, particular, and slightly pushy.

"I'll get the job done," he says, finally glancing my way with annoyance.

I don't want to piss him off.

His touchiness makes him seem flighty.

Breathe, Shay—you're just being paranoid about the time-frame. Everything is fine.

"Great." I make my smile bigger and then turn, rolling my eyes when he can't see me, only to let out an unattractive noise at the truck pulling into The Marina's parking lot.

Of course he's showing up right now.

Of course he's scowling at me through the front wind-shield as he parks.

Of course his dark gaze never leaves mine as he exits his truck.

I swallow, hold my head high, and take a discreet breath.

I have to. Luca Asher is walking toward me, and I have to prepare myself for our personas when we are around each other.

It's what works best.

Especially when he runs his hand through his hair to tuck

back that single brown curl falling over his face. Or when his walk holds such a commanding purpose that I can't pull my eyes away if I tried.

Or the way his simple stupid navy blue Asher Construction T-shirt is tucked into the front of his light wash jeans, revealing his tan belt and showing off how lean and toned his abs are.

You can't actually see them, but my god, are they toned.

Owning a marina means I've seen my share of the town in very little clothing, but Luca—yeah, he's memorable.

In more ways than I'd like to admit.

"What the hell is this, Shay?" He folds his arms in front of his chest and widens his stance.

I mimic him and tilt my head.

Here we go.

"This is me owning and running a business that has nothing to do with you, Luca."

With that, I turn on my heel.

Even if I couldn't hear the crunch of gravel under his boots behind me, I'd know he was following me. My body is constantly aware of Luca when he's nearby.

Traitor.

"You hired someone from out of town. No, no, out of state. You may as well just punch me in the face or something."

"Is that an option?" I ask with more excitement than Luca cares for.

He ignores me, so I continue on inside The Marina. Despite business being slower than it used to be, I do still have a few customers daily.

"Why would you do this?" Luca goes on.

"Again," I begin with a much calmer tone than his and without turning around, "none of your business."

"This town is my business."

Ugh. His loyalty to everyone around him is bullshit.

I know firsthand.

"Don't act like you care about this town and the people in it."

I round the corner to the bar inside The Marina and drop the wooden countertop door to block him from following me back here.

He lifts the counter door and steps right next to me. He clearly didn't get the memo.

I ignore the firm hills of his chest that I feel under my palm as I push him back to the other side.

I drop the door and then look him in the eye.

"I work on this side. You stay on that one."

"Shay, come on. This place is like—"

"A marina to you and nothing more."

His hands land on his hips as he glares at me.

Years ago, I would have fallen under a trance at the fact his ocean-blue eyes are focused on me and only me, but I'm not a silly teenager anymore who follows my brother and his best friend around the lake all summer.

No, I'm a grown woman who knows better.

Luca's voice lowers as he says, "You know that's not true."

For a split second, I swear I hear emotion in his tone. Pleading. But then he steps back and points at me.

"You know this is wrong."

I shake my head.

"I think you can go now."

"Shay, think about it. I know this place. If you want it remodeled to be like it was—because hell, you and I both know this place was the best when we were kids—I'm the right man for the job. Let me help you."

It takes everything in me not to smile or agree with him.

I've had all those same thoughts, but none of that changes our past.

My family would sell this place in a heartbeat if I hired Luca to bring it back to life.

He might be the right man for this job, but he lost that opportunity the day he betrayed my brother, my family, and *me*.

"Goodbye, Luca."

He steps back, our eyes locked as he challenges me to change my mind.

I won't.

I watch him walk away with a growl.

It's easy.

I've been doing it my whole life.

CHAPTER ONE

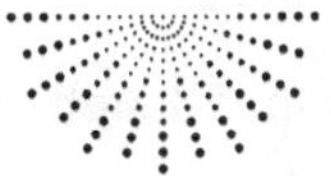

SHAY - PRESENT DAY

"Wait, stop! Please!" I race after Brent, my contractor, as he stalks across The Marina's parking lot in the direction of his truck. His jeans hang low, and the faster he walks, the farther they fall. His shirt is a size too small, which is why I can see how much his jeans are sagging, ready to show me something I really, *really* don't want to see, but who cares about that right now? I need him to stop and listen to me.

"Go! Get on the road!" he yells at one of his employees who's just sitting in his own truck with the window rolled down and his arm hanging out.

His employee taps the side of his truck and then peels out, the tires kicking up rocks and dust.

"Brent, please. I'm sorry. I didn't—"

"For the last year, I've listened to you nitpick everything I do and then proceed to tell me how you think I should do it differently. Blah, blah. It's annoying."

"Well, I am paying you to do it how I want it, but I understand—"

"I'm done. Fucking done, lady. You can keep the material since you already paid for it, but as far as labor, you can do that shit yourself."

Lady. What am I, fifty? I'm only thirty.

He yanks his truck door open, and I step up to it.

"Is this really how you want to conduct business? This is completely unprofessional."

"Me?" he snaps and then laughs wickedly as he starts the engine and, like his employee, peels out. I spin to block the dirt from flying into my eyes. Pieces nick at my bare arms and legs, since I'm only wearing a halter tank top and shorts today. There isn't a lick of wind, and it's nearing ninety.

I'd be walking around in just shorts and my bikini top if there wasn't construction happening. Which, now there isn't.

When I turn back around, The Marina's parking lot is empty and the tailgate of Brent's truck is all I see.

Jackass.

I get it.

But to be fair, it's been a year, and Brent hasn't even finished part one of my plan.

I tried to be patient. He can only send a couple of workers at a time, and I can only afford to let them stay in one of the lodges for free for so long, too. Business is busy everywhere but at The Marina, and everything takes longer with travel time, too.

But screw him. He promised me he'd get the job done, and he just bailed.

Oh god.

He just bailed.

He quit.

My only contractor quit.

"Shit!" I yell and startle when I hear my best friend, Grace, laugh as she stands in The Marina's entrance.

"Is this a new form of therapy?" she asks.

I huff and march toward her.

"Brent just quit."

The smile on her face drops. "You're joking, right?"

I shake my head, push past her into The Marina, and stride right through the mini shop we have until I reach the bar.

Carl is working right now, but he moves on to another area of The Marina when I step behind the bar.

I have three employees as of this moment: Carl, Matt, and Brian. We all share the work between the bar, outdoor food service, the shop, and rentals. Matt is, however, the only cook, so he spends most of his time in the kitchen. I've taken over all the cabin cleanings.

Still, none of them will have a job soon if I don't make a plan fast.

"Shay, you can't afford for him to quit," Grace says.

"I know."

"You need a new plan."

"I know."

I pour myself a glass of water from behind the bar, then refill Grace's soda.

"Any chance you know of another contractor?"

Her face scrunches. "The lodge uses Luca."

Grace's family owns Lovers Lodge. It's what our town is known for, and it brings in tourists all year round for weddings. Multiple magazines have featured them, and they are a thriving business. Like The Marina, they offer boat and jet ski rentals, but it's nothing near what The Marina offers. They aren't competition by any means, but their business definitely helps mine and vice versa, and every day that ticks by is a day my family's business doesn't hold up.

I release a deep sigh, letting my gaze fall to the back wall that's all windows. The mountain background and sun over the glassy lake gives the impression that all is calm in the world.

Everywhere but my head, maybe.

How am I going to fix this?

I perk up. Refusing to wallow, I grab my laptop that's folded up behind the bar's cash register. I don't have time to waste. I need to find a new contractor.

"Are you going to hire out of state again?" Grace asks.

"Maybe, or maybe just from somewhere else in Wyoming. Wind Valley is only a couple of hours away. They have two construction companies. Fingers crossed that one of them has immediate availability."

"I think you need to consider hiring Luca." Grace didn't waste any time sharing her opinion.

"I can't."

"He's right here, and he—"

"You know I can't." I pin Grace with a glare. She's been in my life just as long as Luca and knows our history down to the smallest detail of how once, when I was six, I married two of my stuffed animals, announcing them Luca and Shay Asher after they said I do.

Blah. I was a delusional kid.

"You don't think your family has moved on by now?"

I tilt my head and recall the conversation I had with dear old Mom and Dad last spring.

"You get two summers to turn this place around or we sell

it, and do not under any circumstances hire that Asher boy. Understood?"

Grace grins at my impression of my mother.

"She didn't say that."

"She did. My brother even added that he'd die before he'd trust Luca to help us."

"To be fair, The Marina is like the middle man on why you all hate him."

"He did it to himself."

She holds her hand up.

"You don't have to tell me. I know what happened. I just … has anyone ever asked him about it?"

"My parents did, and he denied everything. Even did this whole act of "I'll help you find who did it," but my parents didn't fall for it."

"Yeah, but what if he actually—"

"He did it, Grace. He's the only other person who knew the passcode."

She nods. "All right, so tell me about your new options for a contractor."

I spin the computer to face her and for the next two hours, we weigh the pros and cons on who I should hire next.

———

MY CELL IS RINGING the moment I walk through my front door at dinnertime.

I pull it from my back pocket and groan. It's my brother's name on the screen.

He's in France with his wife and her family for two more

months, so why does he feel the need to call me every single day? Especially when he's six hours ahead of me and it's nearing ten at night for him. He should be sleeping or something.

I flop back onto my couch, grabbing a magazine to fan my face as I answer the call. The heat of this day never let up.

"Hello, Leo. Let me guess, baby girl isn't sleeping again."

His sigh is loud and clear.

"Not even close. This time change has her so lost, and I told Leslie I'd be on night duty tonight so she could sleep."

Leslie is my brother's wife and the most patient woman I know. Maybe it's because she grew up in France and everything is different there. All I know is that my brother met her the second week of college and they have been together ever since. They live here in Lovers and have three girls now, but with the new baby, they are back in France to see her family for the summer. Both my brother and sister-in-law have remote jobs, so it works for them. My parents are also there because they've never been to Europe. They are making a whole trip of it and will fly back at the end of the summer with Leo and Leslie.

Right now, I'm more than grateful none of them are here to witness my current dilemma.

"That was nice of you."

"Yeah, well, it's the least I could do. It doesn't matter that I've been practicing this language for more than a decade. Leslie does almost all the translations everywhere we go, so we need her to be well-rested."

I let out a slight laugh. My brother really does suck at speaking French.

"How's the trip outside of that?"

"Good. The girls love it here. I think it's more about the

fact that they currently have both sets of grandparents around. Spoiled doesn't even begin to describe how the days go for them."

"They should be spoiled. They are Parker girls. We expect nothing less."

"Don't I know it. Anyway, how's The Marina going?"

"Good," I answer quickly. "Really good."

"I can't wait to see what you've done with it. Is that Brent guy picking up the pace?"

"Mm-hmm," I say. It's not a lie. He sure got to it when he drove out of town.

"That's nice to hear. I was worried when he was still behind schedule as we left."

"Oh, yeah, well, the weather is shaping up again, so we are making better progress."

Now that was a lie.

"I'm glad. I think Mom and Dad are having so much fun that the idea of selling that place is more appealing now that they could start traveling more."

"If they just sold it to me, we could all have what we want," I remind him.

"You know they won't sell to you until they see you turn a profit. They won't sell a failing business to their daughter. You can't blame them for that."

No. I can't. I just don't understand how I left for college and they just let it fall apart. Leo cares about The Marina, but he never dreamed of running it himself one day, and he cares about his family more, which is understandable. Letting him run it while he was starting a family wasn't the right move, but I wasn't around to voice that opinion. No, I was away at school, earning a degree in business, doubling up on courses over the summer to get back here as quickly as possible just so I could run The Marina one day. It's been my plan since I was a kid when my parents would let me help out over the summers in the store or in the restaurant and I saw how happy this place made people. I loved the atmosphere and the people at The Marina. Now, I'm finally here to pick up the pieces and time is running out.

"Shay, did you hear me?"

"What?"

"How much do you think you'll have done before we get back?"

"Enough," I tell him.

"Enough? Shay, it's the first of June. We are coming back in September. You don't have much time."

"I know. You don't have to remind me."

My tone is snappy, but he brings up the deadline at least once a week.

"I'm not trying to bring you down. I just don't want you to waste more time on something that might not make it."

My eyes sting. Not because he's hurting my feelings but more because after today, he might be right.

I have just under four months to make a new plan, execute it, and prove to my parents The Marina is worth saving.

And right now, I seem to be alone in this goal.

CHAPTER TWO

LUCA

What the fuck is happening?

As if it's the most natural thing in the world, I watch as Miles, my twin brother, mind you—clearly twin telepathy or whatever isn't a real thing—places his hand on the lower back of his mortal enemy.

All right, all right. Mortal enemy might be a stretch, but that doesn't change the fact that my brother is cozying up to Quinn Banks right now.

In public.

At our older brother Hudson's bar.

And Miles seems to be enjoying himself.

I'd slap myself if I weren't in so much shock right now.

He can't stand Quinn.

She's … she's … well, there's nothing wrong with her, to be fair, but Miles thinks everything about her is wrong.

Her lifestyle. Her hair. Her smile. Her … shit, yeah, okay, I get it now.

Still, when in the hell did this happen, and how did I miss it?

Miles looks at me quickly but then glances away.

That's right. Don't look me in the eye. I'll know what you're thinking.

In fact, I'll probably—

A truck speeding by the big window that reveals Main Street steals my attention.

Anderson Construction.

What.

The.

Fuck.

I get up abruptly and walk out the door to watch not one, not two, but three trucks go by. They head down Main Street, a lot faster than the speed limit allows, in the direction that leads out of town.

Good.

Bye-bye. Don't let the allegiance of our small town kick you in the ass on your way to the highway.

Assholes.

I still can't believe they accepted a job here anyway.

Loyalty is one of the most important traits a person could have, and the person who hired those greedy fuckers is lacking far more than they'll ever admit.

I can't blame her completely. She's close with her family the way I am with my own. If I were ever in that situation, I'd pick my family too.

The only problem is, I thought that family *was* my family. I mean, I'd spent just as much time at their house as I spent at my own. Our families used to do get-togethers on a weekly basis, but then one day, someone stole from The Marina, and they blamed it on me.

I tried to convince them that I had no idea what they were talking about, because I didn't steal shit, but no one believed me. Yes, it hurts that Shay doesn't believe me, but it hurts more that her brother, Leo, didn't. We did everything together and, well, I considered him just as much my brother as I do Hudson and Miles.

But he didn't believe me either.

It sucked.

A lot.

I wanted to get back at him for not trusting me after all the years of friendship we had, so I slept with his girlfriend. I was a teenager. I was dumb. I was a fucking idiot. Any chance we had to fix our friendship was 100 percent ruined by my one single choice.

That's how quickly your life can change.

And every single day that I see those trucks or I see Shay, I'm reminded of just that.

Now, at least half the problem is gone. The other, well, I guess I just cross my fingers I don't run into her in town.

———

WORK HAS BEEN BUSY, and by the time 4 p.m. hits and I'm sending the guys home, I still have paperwork to complete. Bids to prepare, payroll, and a few mock-up designs to draft.

I wave goodbye to Benson, Darrell, and Stan, my three employees, then lock the shop door to Asher Construction. I'll be back to work in the office, but it's hot as fuck right now, so I need a cold drink and some food.

One of the things I love about living in a small town is that everything is within walking distance. Outside of the lodge and The Marina anyway. My shop is right at the end of Main Street, so I really have a prime spot. If I turn left from the shop, I would hit Restore and Repair, Miles garage, in one block or my dad's house in three and the grocery store in four. If I walk straight, Main Street will lead to Hudson's Bar, B's Bakery, three small restaurants, clothing shops, a new dance studio, a jewelry store, a florist, and a few other basic businesses every town has like a bank, a law office, et cetera. If I turn right, my house is one block over.

Like I said, it's a prime spot.

I walk up Main Street until I reach B's Bakery. Brooke, who owns it, will be closing any moment, if she hasn't already.

The open sign is still showing when I get there, so I swing the door open.

"I know, I know, I do this way too much and you'll have to make a fresh pot of coffee just for—"

I stop mid-sentence and take a misstep. Brooke is not alone.

"Hey, Luca." Brooke smiles and waves from behind the counter. On the side, picking up her coffee, is Grace Richford.

Now, I've known Grace for a long time. Since before we could drive.

My best friend growing up was Leo Parker, and Grace was, still is, Leo's little sister's best friend.

So that means, by Shay's standards, Grace doesn't care for me either.

As soon as Grace spots me, her left brow raises.

Now, it could mean she's displeased to see me, but it could also be due to the fact that I'm just staring at this point.

"Brooke. Grace." I nod to them.

Grace laughs and then flips her hair over her shoulder.

"Luca."

Cool. More awkward silence. My fucking favorite. Not.

"Any chance there's coffee left for me?"

"I had a feeling you'd be in today," Brooke says, and Grace laughs.

Why is she laughing? Brooke didn't say anything funny.

I snap my gaze to Grace, and she rolls her eyes with a smile.

"I'll see you two later," she says and heads for the door.

As soon as she's gone, Broke says, "You could be nicer."

"I'm nice."

"You do business with her family."

"Technically, I work with her brother and not her. We all know how Grace can be."

"Do we, though?" Brooke asks. "Because she's nice to everyone, including you."

"She was just laughing at me."

"No, she wasn't. She was laughing because when she came in asking if I had coffee left, I said yeah, I have a hunch Luca is about to walk in here to ask the same question. And then viola, you did."

"Really?" I feel a bit stupid for assuming.

"Just because Shay doesn't like you doesn't mean Grace doesn't."

Brooke hands me my iced black coffee with cream, and I hand her some cash.

"I actually think you and Grace would get along great. You should ask her out."

Now it's my turn to laugh.

I'll admit, I've considered it, but this is a small town, and as I said before, the family she's closest to hates me.

She'd never go for it.

Which sucks because, again, small towns don't carry a lot of options when it comes to dating.

"Why is that funny?" Brooke asks.

"Because her best friend is Shay, so could you just imagine us all hanging out?"

Brooke sighs. "I guess you're right. Doesn't it bug you though, watching your brother fall in love and … I don't know. Being far from it?"

I study Brooke for a moment, and I'm about to ask her if watching her best friend Sadie and my older brother Hudson fall in love is bothering her, but then the door opens and Grace's older brother, Dutton, walks in.

Brooke marches past me, flips the open sign to closed, and then points at it all while looking at her new customer.

"It didn't say that when I walked in."

"It says it now," she snaps, and I can't help it. My eyes widen because, holy shit, I've never heard Brooke use that snarky tone before.

Dutton shakes his head and then looks up to me.

"I have some work I need done at the lodge. Can you come by later this week?"

I nod. "Tomorrow. I'll be there."

"Thanks," he says and leaves without even looking at Brooke once more.

Another bout of awkward silence fills the bakery as

Brooke locks the door behind him. She huffs and then smiles at me as she heads for the kitchen.

"I guess I'll just go out the back?" I ask. She nods.

Then she's gone, and I'm left standing there.

What is with the people in this town right now?

First Miles is being weird with Quinn, and now Brooke with Dutton. Sure, I don't know Dutton very well. I only know the work side of him, and yeah, it's only two people, but two people who play a very active role in my life.

Damn.

Is it the coffee?

I hold the cup up as if I can see through it and then chuckle to myself.

Maybe I just need to get a life.

I let myself out the back door of the bakery. It would be weird that I'm doing that, but since my older brother is engaged to Brooke's best friend, who used to own the bakery, it's not.

I head toward Hudson's Bar's back door. Again, my brother owns the bar, so it's not that weird.

I wave to his kitchen staff as I walk through, and as soon as I open the door to the main bar, Hudson looks up and smiles. I wave and then my gaze snags on Grace, who is just leaving with a take-out bag in hand.

Seems we both have a busy night ahead of us.

Dating isn't the worst idea, and Grace has her life together, which is nice. She runs her family's lodge with her siblings, and they do well for themselves. Dating another like-minded motivated individual sounds like something I could get on board with. She's smart, driven, lives on her own, and is only a couple of years younger than me. She's perfect on paper.

I sigh and take a seat at the bar. I'll order a burger to go so I can get back to work.

My gaze drifts to Grace once more as she walks by the front window.

Suddenly, Shay comes into view. She looks panicked.

I can't help but grin.

Karma is a good friend right now.

And a good friend is exactly what I'd need from the person I'm dating.

So, that means Grace is out.

The door opens, and Shay walks in.

Our eyes meet, and I groan while she glares.

Looks like I won't be ordering a burger after all, because there's no way I'm sticking around for whatever mood Shay is dishing up.

She may be one of the prettiest women I've ever set my eyes on, but I don't have the time or the energy for a woman like her.

CHAPTER THREE

SHAY

Girls' night is the best night.

Especially right now. I need help, and these women are the only ones who know my secret and have kept it. Hell, our friendship as a whole is basically a secret. It has been since the day I walked into B's Bakery and overheard Sadie planning the layout for Sips and Stories, her bookstore that is attached to Hudson's Bar.

That was almost a year ago this fall, and all it took was the mention of one Meghan Quinn book that we all loved a little too much and we agreed to a secret night to talk about it. Now, that one night has turned into meeting as much as we can with our schedules to talk about whatever we are reading. Turns out, we all find a way to read multiple books a week, and I love it. Small town or big city, readers are everywhere.

I'd headed to Hudson's Bar last night hoping to get advice, but Luca was there and so was Miles and so was—well, way too many people who might gossip.

The last thing I need is any word of who I'm seen in town with getting back to my parents.

Small towns are great, don't get me wrong. But living in a small town where everyone knows that your family, who is well-known, doesn't like another family, who is also well-known, means you have more eyes on you than I care to admit.

I glance over my shoulder as I head up the walkway to my friend Brooke's front door. I don't bother knocking before I step inside and let out a breath.

No, it's not the end of the world if people see me, but it would lead to too many questions and I cannot handle more than one problem at a time.

"You made it!" Sadie Collins, who is engaged to Hudson Asher, says with so much happiness, it's hard not to smile at her welcome. She wraps me in a hug. "I'm so sorry about that last night. I could see that you wanted to talk, but the people in the room made it hard."

"It's fine. I get it. I could just suck it up and tell them to mind their own business."

It's true, I could. But I'm not exactly the kind of girl who likes confrontation, so I just … avoid.

"We all could, but the safe choice would be to make a plan first so that you get to set the story. Otherwise, rumors will fly like confetti at a gender reveal."

Also another great reason to avoid confrontation.

I glance at Brooke and then back at Sadie. "Anything you need to share?"

"No." They laugh in unison. "Unless we want to get to the bottom of this whole Miles and Quinn thing. I mean, do you think he got her pregnant and that's why they decided to just *boom* start dating?"

Sadie laughs at Brooke's theory and shakes her head. "And that right there is how rumors get started. Miles is smart, so is Quinn. Whatever is going on with them is their problem, not mine, not yours, and definitely not Shay's."

"Agreed. So what is Shay's problem?" Brooke asks, nodding to the living room for us to move there. Just as we sit with a charcuterie board and mimosas, Grace blasts through the door.

"Sorry, sorry, a last-minute reservation got lost and my brother couldn't find it and it was chaos. What did I miss?"

She drops her purse to the floor along with a pair of slippers in her hand, toes off her heels, and replaces them with the fuzzy ones.

We might be a small town, but seeing as how Grace runs the lodge and its status is growing larger in the country, if she's working, she will never not be wearing heels.

It's crazy how we ended up as best friends. I'm in torn jean shorts and a tank with slip-ons, and she's all business.

"Shay was about to give us an update on The Marina."

"Oh, good. Tell her to hire Luca."

"For what?" Sadie grabs a cracker with cheese.

"Her contractor bailed yesterday," Grace says for me.

"Oh my god."

"Are you freaking kidding?"

I groan and down my first mimosa.

"It's true, and if I don't find someone to replace him soon, that's it. I'll lose The Marina."

"Oh, babe." Sadie hugs me.

Brooke refills my drink and says, "Would hiring Luca be the worst?"

"Absolutely, it would." I grab a cheese cube and toss it into my mouth.

"That would basically seal The Marina's fate. The moment word gets out that he and I are working together, my parents would have Linc stake a for sale sign out front faster than the speed of light."

"I would tell my brother he can do no such thing," Sadie says. Her family owns the only reality company in Lovers.

Again. Small-town things.

"I'd steal it every night just so they'd have to replace it, and eventually they'd run out and take it as a sign that they can't sell."

We all turn to Grace, who has never looked more serious.

"Damn, Richford. Really?"

She nods.

I grin proudly at my friend's secret rebel side.

"I just think, you know, he does good work. He's efficient. He could probably still get everything done on your timeline, too."

"Brooke," I groan. "I can't."

"Okay, okay, watching him work would be a plus, too. Those hot summer days. Does he ever work shirtless?"

"Why are you looking at me?" Sadie asks with a laugh.

"He helped build the bookstore."

"That you own a business right next to. Have you ever seen him work shirtless?"

"No. But it wasn't summer either."

Grace laughs. "He is pretty fit."

"Fit," I repeat and then gag, sticking a finger in my mouth for emphasis.

"Girl, you can hate the man all you want, but you have to admit that he's nice to look at." Grace drinks her mimosa.

I roll my eyes, but I'm smiling and nodding.

He really is.

I'll admit it.

That might be what I dislike most about him.

That and the fact that these girls are right, he really would be the perfect person for this job. I've seen his work all over town. I know how quickly he works while still delivering high-quality results.

I take another sip, listening to the girls start to talk about our latest book.

None of it changes the fact that I can't hire Luca, even if my mind keeps straying to how it could work.

My parents would flip if they found out.

I reach for the salami.

If.

If they found out.

If.

The word repeats itself all night long.

In fact, two mimosas later, I'm starting to believe I can still make my dreams come true.

If I can convince Luca to agree to it.

Fingers crossed.

CHAPTER FOUR

LUCA

I'm pretty sure that Miles is lying to me.

He's never lied to me.

Ever.

Till now.

And I can't even focus on it completely because Sandhill Contractors, a company out of Wind Valley, had a truck roll through town first this morning. They were headed for The Marina.

It's absolute bullshit.

"Hey, whoa, what did that door do to you?"

I look up to see my dad sitting in the lobby of my shop.

"Hey, Dad." I let out a deep breath. "Sorry."

"It's not my shop, but just because you could fix the door yourself if you break it doesn't mean you should."

I nod and then point at my office.

The guys will all be coming back soon. It's another scorcher out there today, so I told them to cut out early. I don't need anyone getting heat stroke on me. The work can wait if it means safety for my guys. It also means a more hands-on approach from me to help where I can and keep everything on schedule.

"What brings you in today?" I ask.

Dad doesn't normally make random appearances at work like this, seeing as how I'm a grown man and all. It reminds me of when I was a kid. A teenager, to be more specific. He knew instantly when something was bothering me and would just appear in the doorway of my bedroom. It must be a parent instinct thing, and my dad's sense for it only heightened after my mom passed away. I was fifteen and everything about it sucked. Dad made it his goal to make sure we all knew how much we were loved after it happened, and to this day, given how he studies the expression on my face, the love this man has for his kids hasn't changed.

"Just checking in to see how my youngest boy is doing."

"One minute, Dad, doesn't make me the youngest.

"Eh, technically it does."

"Dad."

"Luca."

"Why are you here?"

"I saw the truck this morning, too, and just wanted to see how you were."

"Honestly, I don't care."

"Not even a little?"

"Nope."

"So you're ready to see them every single day while they work on The Marina."

"Are you kidding me?" I stand quickly, and some paper flies off my desk. "She hired him on the spot?"

"Ah, so you care a little."

I narrow my gaze on my dad, but he just chuckles.

"I did raise you, you know. I know you."

I make some weird grunting noise and sit back down.

"Why don't you go talk to Shay? Make an offer."

"I did. Last summer, and she told me to fuck off."

"Luca Asher," Dad scolds.

"Sorry."

He hates it when we curse.

"She told me to leave multiple times, and because she's a fine and kind lady, I listened and skedaddled."

Dad chuckles.

"Much better. Thank you."

I can't help it. I laugh, too, and instantly feel lighter, thanks to him.

I wasn't kidding when I said family is important to me. Trust is important. And it's probably a good thing Shay won't hire me, because trust is not something she and I have in each other.

"Why don't you just apologize for whatever it was that happened all that time ago and move forward?"

I nod.

I never told my family what happened. Not even Miles. I was, and still am, ashamed of my side of it, so not telling them any of it seemed easier. Plus, a part of me thought it might all blow over, and I didn't want there to be a rift between the parents. They were friends, too.

It never blew over, and Dad lost, too.

It kills me that I played a part in that.

"I'll think about it," I tell him and then look away. I can see in his eyes that he wants me to say more.

"Good. That's a good plan."

He stands to hug me and then leaves.

I hear the guys as they return to the shop to drop their things off and then as they all leave. I take that as my cue to fill a cooler with water and ice and go check on the sites. Asher Contraction is currently hired for six projects. Anything from a new deck on Mrs. Whittaker's back porch to the new house for the elementary school principal.

I grab a fresh stick of sunscreen before I walk out the door. A man can never be too prepared for the rays of that afternoon sunshine.

———

MY FACE IS BURNED.

Figures.

I reapplied and yet, my nose already hurts to touch.

I step into Hudson's Bar around seven and practically groan with pleasure as the air-conditioner assaults me.

If it wouldn't cause a scene, I'd whip my shirt off right now and really soak the cool air in.

I close my eyes and drop my head back.

It's heaven here. Now I just need a beer, maybe a club sandwich, and some—

"Are you going to move or continue to stand there and stink the place up?"

My groan instantly shifts from pleasure to annoyance.

I'm ready to relax for the night, not bicker with Shay.

Someone laughs next to her, and my eyes spring open.

Grace.

I step back, holding my hand out as if to say, *please, right after you.*

"Wow. Silence. So your mouth does know how to do something besides speak."

Shay takes one step, then I step up behind her, my lips right next to her ear. "My mouth knows how to do a lot of things besides talk, Shay."

She gasps, spinning to me with wide eyes.

Her lips part, and I don't know if it's the long day, the heat is hindering my thoughts, or the way her eyes shine as she looks at me, but my brain sends the signal for me to kiss her.

It's fucking weird.

And hot.

I clear my throat and step back at the same time she does, my words repeating in my mind.

My mouth knows how to do a lot of things besides talk, Shay.

I said that. To Shay Parker.

Wow.

Here I was worried about my boys being in the heat for too long, and look at me now.

I've gone mad.

"What's happening?" Grace asks, tugging Shay's arm.

Shay just shakes her head, and then they walk off toward the bar.

I do the same, but in the opposite direction.

"Beer?" Hudson asks after I take a seat.

"Beer."

He sets my usual on the bar then quickly makes drinks for Shay and Grace. They take them and snag a spot by the open windows where Hudson set up fancier seating last summer when Sadie first moved in with him.

As if she hears me thinking about her, Sadie steps behind the bar to help Hudson.

How fucking wild would it be to lose your memory? I'd say one in every ten times I look at Sadie, I think about what it must have been like for her. Then I see the way she looks at my brother.

What a trip that was. Now they're engaged.

"Are you eating dinner here tonight?" Sadie steps in front of me.

"Yeah."

I glance over my shoulder. Miles usually pops in around this time, but he's not here.

"Have you seen Miles?"

Sadie shakes her head. "Not today, sorry."

Hudson was this way when he was first officially with Sadie, too.

I guess it's just me tonight.

Loud laughter catches my attention, and I find myself looking at Shay once again.

She looks pretty tonight. Her hair is down, and she's wearing a little pink sundress instead of her usual tank and jean shorts.

Not that I have her wardrobe memorized or anything. It's just … a small-town thing, I think.

Grace, too, is cute in her pantsuit outfit. It's actually a little intimidating. Would she wear that on a date?

Should I ask her on a date?

It'd beat sitting here in the bar eating dinner alone.

I nod.

As soon as Shay leaves, I'll ask Grace to dinner.

I take another bite of my sandwich and find my gaze searching for Shay once more.

I track her every step as she walks toward the door.

It's weird that I watched her grow from this kid to a teenager. I was there every single day, and then one day I wasn't, and now here she is, all woman.

A woman who pisses me off on the daily and has me even more pissed now that she hired another out-of-towner.

I let out a breath and finish my dinner, eating as if I haven't eaten in days. After another beer, I pay my tab and look for Grace.

She's just placing her purse strap over her shoulder as she heads for the door.

I hop off my stool quickly.

"Grace, wait up," I call out and follow her. She pushes the door open slowly as she looks at me.

"Hey, Luca. Is everything okay?" she asks.

"Yeah." I glance around the bar, and then I nod for us to step outside.

We let the bar door close, and I decide to just blurt it out before I can think twice.

"Would you want to go to dinner with me sometime?"

Her mouth hooks into a smile.

"Like a date?"

I nod. "Yes."

Her smile quickly straightens, and she sighs.

"I … you're really sweet, Luca, and we'd probably have a good time, but I'm best friends with Shay. You and her brother … the history here … I just think it would be complicated. I'm sorry."

Well fuck.

That's embarrassing.

"Right. Yes. Yeah, that would be… tricky." I blow out a breath. "Well, enjoy your night."

"You too." She reaches out for me, her hand rubbing my forearms as if I'm a child who needs comforting. "I really am sorry."

"It's all good," I reassure her and then wave, stepping back so that I can head home and die a little from embarrassment inside the safety of my own house. "Good night."

"Night, Luca."

I turn and head home, walking a little faster than normal.

I called it and asked anyway.

Stupid.

No.

What's stupid is the fact that Grace said no because Shay and her family don't care for me.

The lights over my garage door light up as I turn to walk up my driveway. I enter the code to open the garage, but before I duck inside, I spot a gift by the front door.

It's flowers from Mrs. Whittaker for letting her tell me stories about her late husband while I worked tonight.

See. This is the shit I'm talking about. The people of Lovers are loyal, and then you have the Parker family doing the opposite.

I let out a breath and close my eyes.

It's not even about Grace turning me down just now.

I'll lose my mind if Shay hires another out-of-state or even out-of-town company to finish the job.

If I were smart, I'd go to her and pitch my own idea to get

the job, but I'm not an idiot. I'd be wasting my time, because it's clear that hiring me isn't an option for her. Ever.

I set the flowers in the garage and then stomp to the mailbox.

It's been years. Years.

I don't know which pisses me off more: the fact she won't hire me or the fact that her family still holds a grudge. I mean, can I blame them? I'm still obsessing over why they won't forgive me, so maybe I hold one, too.

I flip through the envelopes, stopping in the middle of my driveway as a small purple one comes into view. It's not your typical piece of mail. No, this one just says my name in all capital letters and has no return address or stamp, which means someone went out of their way to put this in my box.

Hell, for all I know, I'm going to open it and glitter will pop out, covering me head to toe.

I'll take my chances though, because this handwriting looks vaguely familiar.

My curiosity gets the best of me.

I rip open the back and pull out the note.

MEET me tonight behind the old boat toy shack. Wait till the Main Street lights dim, and do not tell a single person where you're going. I mean it.

I CHUCKLE.

This has to be Shay. There is literally not another soul in this town who would be this dramatic in a letter. Or one who wants to be sure no one sees the two of us together.

This has to mean one thing. She's desperate and ready to hire me.

The question is … am I ready to say yes and let her boss me around?

CHAPTER FIVE

SHAY

I'm going to puke.

I can feel it. It's right there, ready to creep up my throat. My skin feels clammy, and it's so freaking hot out here.

Shit.

I can't believe I'm really going to do this. I'm going to hire Luca Asher to remodel The Marina. If my family could only see me now, they would be so disappointed.

But I'm desperate and his work is good. I just don't know how to make this work without anyone seeing us, but I'll find a way. I have to.

I sit down on the bench and then I stand up and then I sit down again, my hands twisted together as I look left and right, making sure there's no one in sight.

Where is he?

I know I was a little vague in my note, but he surely knew it came from me.

I sit back down on the bench and look out over the water.

I picked this spot because in a moment when I'm feeling so unsure of what's going to happen next, this view calms me.

I let out a breath.

If somewhere deep down—deep, deep down—Luca is still the Luca I knew years ago, he's going to say yes because, as he mentioned last summer when I hired the other company, he knows this place. He knows the memories I want to keep alive, and he knows the vision I have to make it what it once was. His brain is scarily similar to mine. That's what drew me to him all those years ago.

It's just that no one can find out about this, and I can't stress this enough.

If I don't get The Marina back up and running, I could lose it. If my family finds out I hired Luca, I could lose it.

That's the part I don't know if Luca is going to agree to.

What's the saying? Play with fire and you'll get burned.

Yep. That's me. I'm basically walking around with the gasoline clenched in my hand and a match in the other, waiting for someone to bump into me.

"I think I finally see why this is your favorite spot around the lake."

I startle at Luca's voice, standing quickly and spinning around to face him. My gaze jerks to his instantly, then he breaks eye contact to take me in, his eyes traveling down and back up my body so slowly that I feel naked. When those blue eyes meet mine again, I can see that he has questions for me. I expected it.

"Why is that?" I ask.

"Because this view is like a sedative. The entire drive here, I was building up a fight in my head with you because that's what we do, but then I got out of my truck and saw this"

—he gestures to where the sun barely peeks out from behind the lake and mountains as it goes down for the night—"and the anger just disappeared."

I have to fight back the smile on my lips. His assumption is perfect.

But I don't smile. Right now, I can't show any signs that Luca Asher holds the cards.

"How can you plan a fight with someone if you don't even know what they want from you?" I ask, and instantly he points a finger at me.

"Because I knew you wanted something from me, and my brain can't figure out one single reason why you think I'd give you anything."

"Because you love that marina just as much as I do," I snap and then sit with a huff.

The lake sand is soft, so I don't hear him as he walks up to me, but I can feel it. So when he sits down next to me and lets out a breath, I know I have only one chance to get this right.

"The Marina isn't doing well, and I thought hiring someone to help me fix it up and rebuild it to what it once was would be the answer, and I still think it is. I just ..."

"They quit on you."

I nod.

"Why?"

I shrug.

"Shay."

I hate that after all these years, he can still tell when I'm keeping something from him.

"He was taking his time and I need it done. I needed him to work faster. It shouldn't take this long."

"That's what you get for hiring out of state."

"Don't start this."

"No, I will start it. I want to know why you hired them over me, because it sure as hell isn't because of my work. You know damn well that I'm great at what I do, and you wouldn't be here right now telling me about this if you weren't planning to hire me. So why now? My guess is desperation, but I'll let you tell me the truth."

"Can't you just be happy that I didn't hire someone else again?"

"Not a chance. Tell me why."

"Because."

"Because why?"

"Because I don't trust you! And my family would be furious with me if I put the fate of this place into your hands."

I toss my own hands up as if to say, *are you happy now?*

Luca jerks his head back, his heated stare locked on me. His jaw clenches as he takes a deep breath, but those eyes, even as they darken, never leave mine.

Why is it that whenever Luca looks at me, I feel like he's seeing more than just what's on the surface? It's like he's trying to see deeper. Like he's trying to know my every thought.

As I wait with bated breath for him to say something in response to my outburst, a breeze sweeps over us, sending goose bumps over my arms and legs. I shiver, and my nipples harden. And clearly, Luca knows it, too, because he looks down.

It's only for a split moment before he stands and starts to walk off.

I'd be mad that he was so bluntly checking out my breasts just now, but I really do need his help, and if I let him leave, I won't have the chance to ask him again. Let alone the nerve.

"Where are you going?" I ask, standing to follow.

"Home."

"Why?"

"Because this was stupid. I don't know why I even entertained this idea tonight."

"No. Wait. Please, Luca, I need your help."

He spins quickly and takes two long strides until he's right in my face.

"You just said that you didn't trust me and your family would be furious. Those two things are a recipe for disaster. Everyone would see me at The Marina and know I'm working with you. I think you forget how small this town is and how everyone knows more than they should about the people who live here. Your family might be across the world right now, but someone would tell them."

"I know. I know. But you wanted me to tell you why I didn't hire you first, and I did. Now you're mad because I told you the truth. That's not fair."

He huffs out a breath.

"And—" I swallow the lump in my throat, then force the next piece out. He's going to hate it. "You'd only be working at night so no one could see you."

"Ha!" He erupts into a wicked laugh. "Now I know why you wanted to meet me at this time. So you wouldn't be seen with me. Unreal."

He turns for his truck again.

"Luca, I'm begging you. Please help me finish The Marina. Please. That place is my *home*."

Like before, he stops. This time though, he doesn't turn

around. He rests his hands on his hips and drops his chin to his chest.

I take one more step, but I don't speak.

Slowly, he looks over his shoulder.

"Please," I beg one more time before he can turn me down again.

"I …"

"I'll do anything you want. Name your price. Do you want me to get you more work in town? I'd find a way to slip your name into conversation."

"I don't need your help with work."

"I'll clean your house."

He closes his eyes and shakes his head.

"I'll … I'll … what do you like?" I ask with a small laugh. "I'm serious, Luca."

"I don't think this is a good idea, Shay. I'm sorry."

"Wait, I … I'll set you up with someone."

I don't know where that came from or why I thought it was a good idea to say out loud, but it's out before I can stop it.

"I don't need your help getting a date," he snaps.

Fair enough.

"Okay. I just figured with your brothers falling in love and whatnot, you'd be ready to do that, too, and if there is someone you are interested in, I could help maybe."

Oh. My. God. Shay. Stop. Talking.

Set the only man you ever had feelings for up on a date? Come on. Those feelings might be different now, but I'm not an idiot. Then again, this was my idea, so maybe I am.

"But you're right." I wave a hand to signal that we can both forget it. "You don't—"

"Grace," he says quickly.

Grace?

"What about her?"

"You can help me with Grace. Given our family histories, she's never given me the time of day, but she seems ..."

"Not your type," I blurt out because clearly I love to sabotage myself.

"You don't know my type."

"I know hers."

"And I'm not it?"

"No."

His glare cuts off my laugh.

"I could be, but she barely speaks to me because your family has probably poisoned her mind all these years."

"Yes, Luca, we just sit around the dinner table every Monday night, passing garlic bread and sharing how much we hate you."

He points his finger at me, and I don't know what it is about the gesture, but I want to smack him and tell him to stop.

"That right there is why, even if we did agree to this, it wouldn't work. I'm leaving."

"No, no, no." I run in front of him. "I'm sorry. Okay. You're right. Grace's image of you might be a little skewed because of me and my brother, so my answer is yes. I'll help set you up with Grace."

"No, that's not what I want. I can get a date myself. What I need from you is for you to say nice things about me so she can form her own opinion of me. A better one. Not the Parker family's opinion, okay? Got it? I'll do the rest."

I nod over and over.

He's saying yes, and all I have to do is say nice things about him to my best friend. Easy. Done.

"But make sure it's things she would like, not stupid stuff like his hair was nice today and he smells so good I want to lick his body."

I snort, and it earns me another glare.

"No stupid comments about how pretty you look. Got it."

He rolls his eyes. "Don't make me regret this."

"I won't. See you tomorrow night. Wait until after eight before you show up, and don't bring a trailer."

"How do you expect me to get anything done if I don't have supplies?"

"Tomorrow will be more of a let's make a plan moving forward kind of night."

"Let's just do that now."

"No. Tomorrow," I say and head for my car.

"I think I know why the other guy quit."

The urge to flip him my middle finger consumes me, but he just agreed to help me, so I do the next best thing. Kill him with kindness.

I turn and give him my best smile.

"See you tomorrow."

I unlock my car and grab the handle to open the door.

"No, don't be all sweet with me now. I don't want fake Shay. I want—"

I shut the door and wave at him through the front window, having no idea what more he said.

His hands fly up into the air, and then he shakes his head and gets in his truck.

I wait for him to pull away, and as soon as he does, it's like I can finally breathe.

With my head leaned back against the headrest, I close my eyes.

This is good. It's good. The Marina will be in good hands because Luca is good at his job.

This is going to work.

When I open my eyes, my gaze drifts to where Lovers Lodge sits about two miles down the lake. It's so big that I can see the lights that showcase the structure's character.

Tell Grace nice things about Luca. That's it.

That seems easy enough, right?

But what if I say nice things and she really does deem him her type and then he asks her out and she falls for him and I have to watch my best friend and the only boy I've ever loved be happily in love?

Ugh. I hate how that doesn't sit well with me.

And it's not that I still like Luca. I can't like Luca. It would be pointless.

Which is exactly why I don't.

Like him.

Nope.

Not me.

CHAPTER SIX

LUCA

I didn't sleep very well last night for obvious reasons. Then I started drinking coffee way too soon in my day, pouring a new cup at almost every work location I popped into, because no matter who the job is for, the client always offers me and my guys coffee or food.

We always take it, too.

Maybe the extra caffeine and carbs will be good for me.

I don't even want to start wrapping my mind around the things Shay wants me to do at The Marina. The day is only partially over and I can tell it's going to be a long night.

I wish she would have given me a hint last night. Maybe even an update of where the last guy left off. Is it just the main room, the cabins, what? How quickly does she want this done? What's her plan?

I should have asked so many more questions, but I was honestly still a little shocked that she was finally seeking me out.

It might have short-circuited my brain a touch.

Part of me is excited to see how she plans to update the place. To see what she didn't want me to see for the last year. I'm even more excited that I finally get to be a part of it.

That place holds as much history for me as it does for her.

I park my truck in front of Hudson's Bar and lock it before I go inside to get a late lunch. Half the week, I go home for lunch and the other half, I come here. Work and life schedules don't really give my brothers and me much time to spend together, so this is how I like to make it work.

Sure, we meet on Sundays for breakfast with our dad, but this is different.

Today should have been one of the days I went home. I should have made food real quick and then attempted a nap.

Ha.

A nap.

Like most grown adults, I can't remember the last time I took one of those that wasn't because I was hungover.

I have no idea how late I'm going to be working at The Marina, but if I can't show up until the sun starts to set, then I would imagine it'll be midnight before I get home.

I grab my beer and step outside onto Main Street.

Should I be drinking a beer right now? Probably not, but I'm off work until I meet Shay, so why not relax a little with uno beer?

It's the town's summer festival this afternoon and evening, and even though I have question after question for Miles right now after he showed up with Quinn, I can't think straight.

Sure, I want to know more than what he told me the other day at the gym, but right now, I need to have some type of plan for my own life.

How the hell am I going to do a remodel during the night?

My tools will be loud. I'll need to haul some supplies out there to use at some point.

I sip my beer as my gaze sweeps over the people of Lovers.

My dad is walking down the street, talking to Mrs. Whittaker. Hudson, Sadie, her brother Linc, and Brooke are sitting at a table with Miles and Quinn.

Maybe I should focus on my brother. Hell, it's a great distraction from my own life. My brain is messed up right now. I'm so desperate for work at The Marina that I agreed to do the job in secret all so Shay would put in a good word with her best friend. So I could get a little redemption in the eyes of the woman who turned me down.

Fuck.

That sounds pathetic.

Am I sad that she turned me down, or am I pissed because of her reason why?

"Hey, Luca."

I spin to my right where, as luck has it, Grace is walking toward me.

"Grace," I say, but that's it. Instead, I hold up my drink like I'm cheering her on, and she laughs. She doesn't have a drink in her hand, so I'm sure I look like a fool.

Maybe that's the real reason she said no.

The door to the bar opens and Shay appears, a mixed drink in a can in each hand. Her steps slow as she makes eye contact with me and hands one of the beverages to Grace.

She looks from me to her friend and back, and I immediately want to scream *stop being so fucking obvious*. She's making this weird face with her eyeballs bouncing around like that.

I'm trusting her to help me, and until now, I never thought that maybe she might sabotage me instead as soon as she gets what she wants.

Shit.

Maybe I need to lay some ground rules when we get to work tonight.

"Luca," Shay says, and there is so much disgust in her tone, I'm surprised she didn't actually vomit as she spoke.

I don't even greet her. I just glare and then turn my focus back to Grace.

My lips part to say something, but she beats me to it.

"Wow. Will you two ever grow up?" Grace says. "See you around, Luca."

And then she walks off, leaving me and Shay alone.

Well … that … was …

"What the fuck, Shay?"

"Me?"

Oh, she's going to pretend that it wasn't her arrival to the conversation that lowered Grace's opinion of me more than it was before. This is not my fault.

"Yes, you."

"Do not blame me for your lack of manners, Luca."

"I have manners, Shay."

"Yeah, right, they are just beaming with light right now, Luca."

"They were before you showed up, Shay."

"Stop saying my name after every sentence, Luca."

"You stop."

"No, you stop."

"Oh fuck, we're proving her point," I snap and then toss back my beer.

When I'm finished, I glance at Shay because, to be honest, I'm stunned that she's still here.

Her eyes are on my throat, but as soon as she senses that I'm watching her, those golden irises flicker to mine.

"You're still coming tonight, right?"

"I said I would, didn't I?"

"Well, yeah, but we can't even be around each other for sixty seconds without fighting."

"Looks like we need to figure it out."

I move to walk away, but she reaches out, her slight hand wrapping around my wrist to stop me.

A rush of heat flashes through my body.

I jerk my hand back, my heart racing.

"Don't come too early," she says. Her tone is the one she uses with everyone but me. Between that and the way my body just reacted to her touch, I'm off balance.

Because I'm not sure how to respond maturely, as Grace put it, I lean forward to whisper in her ear.

"Now, now, Shay, that's my line."

She sucks in a breath, her attention now focused on my lips.

Fuck. She's doing it again.

And when she looks at me like she is right now, my brain thinks we need to respond. Grab her, kiss her, push her against the brick building and press my body against hers just to feel the touch of her slender fingers holding on to me.

I don't know how to respond to Shay when she's anything but snappy or witty.

But then someone walks by and bumps her shoulder, pulling her from the trance she'd fallen into, and she huffs.

"You wish."

She walks off before I can say another word.

Which is fine. Honestly, I'm not sure where that conversation could have gone outside of becoming awkward anyway.

I pop back into Hudson's Bar and set my empty glass down then head back outside. This time, I'm greeted with kids running around and tourists from the lodge chatting about how they can't wait to get back out on the water before the sun goes down.

It's a fresh reminder that no matter what issues Shay and I have, returning The Marina to its full potential is a common goal. Sure, I don't own it and won't profit from its success, but my work will be everywhere people look in that place, and someday when I have my own family, I'll be proud to take them there. It will hold different memories than it does now.

That's the goal here.

I need to find a way to push past this thing with Shay.

And I need to find a way in just about five hours.

———

THERE ISN'T a single vehicle in The Marina's parking lot when I pull up. They've been closed for about an hour now, so it makes sense, but still, sometimes a car or a truck might linger for the night because someone made the right choice not to drink and drive.

I'm guessing everyone is at the festival, so business wasn't booming tonight.

Still, the point is, Shay can't scold me for this one.

I slide out of my truck, grabbing some tools from the back before I head inside. I glance around to be sure no one sees me. Which is stupid because we are adults and this is business, but I know how badly Shay's family can hold a grudge, and despite everything, I don't want her to ever be on the receiving end of that.

I set my things down by the door and return to my truck.

It feels weird driving my personal truck, but all the others have Luca's Construction printed on them.

"Hurry up," a high whisper comes from behind me as I reach my driver's door.

I glance over my shoulder. Shay has changed from her festival outfit to a pair of cut-off jean shorts and a tank top. She's barefoot as she stands in the doorway, waving for me to hurry up.

I grab what I left in the truck and meet her at the door.

"I brought you coffee," I tell her as I step inside to check out the space. "I wasn't sure how you took it, so there's a variety of sugars and cream in my lunch box."

"I drink my coffee black, thanks."

Of course she does. Just like her soul.

"I see you didn't bring a trailer or anything. Are we not working right away?"

What the—? Is she being serious right now?

"You told me not to bring one."

"I didn't think you'd actually listen."

"Well, I did. But it's fine. I need to take measurements and notes, and we need to get a plan in place. I need to know your vision, timeframes, and whatnot. Plus, all my trailers have the company name on them, sooooo ..."

"Ah. I didn't think of that."

"Of course you didn't."

"Ugh, is this really how it's going to be for us?"

"Unfortunately, I think so."

She rolls her eyes and points to the room just past the bar.

It's clear this part of The Marina has been well cared for and odd things have been replaced over the years, so the bar area doesn't need to be remodeled the way the dining room and outside deck do.

"I think we need to start with that room. At this rate, maybe finishing one at a time so I can slowly reopen different areas is best. The whole grand reveal isn't part of the plan anymore. Plus, the cabins still need to be updated once the main room is done." She looks defeated as she speaks, but then she smiles. "Despite you being the one to help me, I can't wait to see this place when it's done. Let's go."

She walks away, ready to get to work.

It's obvious that Shay and I don't see eye to eye on just about everything in our lives, but this place is different.

So instead of coming up with some quick comeback the way I normally do, I follow her and get to work.

It's going to be a long night if I want to get all the measurements in this room done so I can plan for tomorrow night.

———

AN HOUR LATER, I've finished measuring everything I need. Now, I'm comparing it to the notes the last contractor left behind, all while Shay hovers over me. She's been watching me since the moment I stepped into this room, and the only reason I haven't told her to get out and let me work is because occasionally she takes pictures of things and then plays on her phone, so I assume she's running through new ideas. Plus, she hasn't said a word to me, and that's been pretty damn nice.

It also proves that we can be in a room together and not fight.

Who would have thought, huh? Not me.

I check off another measurement and sigh. The guy she hired is turning out to be a total moron.

"Oh my god, Luca, if you sigh one more time, I'm going to scream."

"Scream then. I might like it."

Her gaze snaps to me as I grin.

"Just. Stop. Sighing."

I cross my arms and challenge the glare she's giving me.

"Don't you even want to know why I'm doing it?"

"Not really."

"You should."

"Then tell me."

Good to know that even after much-needed silence, we haven't lost our touch.

I step toward her, and she backs up.

I roll my eyes and wave my clipboard in front of her.

She takes a beat to think it over, and then she comes to stand by my side. The smell of cherries, like the super sweet ones you put in drinks, surrounds me.

Damn. She smells good.

"What am I looking at?" she asks, interrupting my internal compliment.

I point to all my check marks where the measurements I just took aren't the same as before.

"See, it's a good thing I remeasured this. He was off by eight to ten inches in just this one spot."

"So."

"So?" I ask, baffled at her casualness to this huge error. "That's a big deal."

"Ten inches isn't that big of a deal."

I gasp. "It's a big deal to me."

"Of course it is."

"What does that mean?"

"It means you're a guy. Eight or ten inches means a lot to you."

I cross my arms.

"Are we still talking about the remodel?" I ask.

She mirrors my stance.

"What else would we be talking about?"

"Well, by the smirk on your face, I'd say right now we're talking about the size of a dick, Shay."

I expect my blunt comment to put her off her game, but it does the complete opposite.

She laughs.

She laughs so hard she snorts.

I'd smile if this weren't a topic I'd dreamed of arguing and winning with a woman someday.

"Okay, I'll bite." She grins. "Ten inches for the rebuild doesn't seem like that big of a deal, but ten inches in bed, preferred."

Her gaze meets mine with another challenge.

My next words are important. They'll be the basis of the entire argument. An argument that isn't going to get very far because, is she fucking serious right now?

"You want a ten-inch cock, Shay, I'll get you a ten-inch cock."

I grab my phone and open the internet.

"What are you doing?" She tries to peek at my screen.

"Aww, that's cute. You have to order me one because yours is too small."

The hand with the phone drops to my side as I turn to face her. I rush forward, so close that she has no choice but to back up until her backside hits the wall. She sucks in a breath when my body presses into hers. The smell of sawdust and cherries consumes me as I lean into her. I position myself so close that our noses touch, and the moment my eyes see the need and want that fills her dark eyes, there is no controlling the words that fall from my lips.

"If you want to know how big my cock is, Shay, all you have to do is ask. It might not be ten inches, but it'll make you feel so fucking full that you won't just be screaming my name when your pussy shatters around it, you'll be begging me for more."

Her lips part as she sucks in a breath, and I swear to god, her hips move forward to brush against mine. She closes her eyes for a millisecond. Long enough for me to quickly run through the consequences of kissing her right now.

But before I can think too hard about it, her eyes pop open and she pushes me back.

"Well, now that you've got the correct measurements, I take it this means we can get started with actual work, right?"

She steps around me and crosses her arms as she looks around the room. At what, I'm not sure. She's looking everywhere but at me, which is fair.

I might have just crossed a line by stepping into her space. If she calls me out on it, I won't argue.

"Yeah, we can get to work."

For the next hour, we confirm plans on this room specifically, and we agree on what I should plan to bring with me tomorrow night.

When I leave, it's just around eleven. Not as late as I expected, but still much later than I usually work.

I back out of the parking lot, and just as I turn the wheel to drive away, I catch sight of Shay walking down the road to her house.

I know it's not far, and I shouldn't give a shit after the way we treat each other, but I still wait, watching until she reaches her front door.

After all, I might say inappropriate things and I argue with her nonstop, but at the end of the day, I'm nothing but a gentleman.

I chuckle.

I'd love to hear Shay's reaction to that.

CHAPTER SEVEN

SHAY

For the record, I'm well aware that ten inches is far too big for a dick.

My heart hurts just thinking of it.

But you know what doesn't hurt? That spot between my legs as I think about what Luca said to me. No, it's not just what he said. It was the confidence in how he said it, in the way his hungry eyes were looking into mine. By the way my body was ready to submit to him had he pushed for more. The way my body gravitated toward him as if it were the most natural thing in the world.

The way I have never, in my entire life, felt so needy for a man the way I felt in that moment.

Shit.

I blow out a breath and spot Grace at The Marina bar as soon as I walk in. I love a lot of things about living in Lovers, but having my best friend live near me and eat breakfast with me each morning here is a top three. We get so busy every day, knowing I'll see her for even ten minutes makes my heart happy.

Good friends are hard to find, and I have one of the best.

"Morning," I greet her and hold my head high. It's time to push all thoughts of Luca Asher and his bedroom talk from my mind.

Oh god, does he talk like that all the time? Even during sex?

I bet that would be … wow. Good. Really, really good.

"You with me?" Grace waves a hand in front of my face.

"Yep."

"Okay, so tell me how night number one went with the enemy."

The enemy, right. His name is Luca. Who I'm supposed to say nice things about to Grace. True things. I can do this. In fact, if it works out for him and they hit it off, I can wash myself free of these thoughts of him.

I should tell her that there is a chance he whispers filthy words during sex.

I open my mouth to do exactly that, but then it occurs to me that it could lead to questions, and, well, how would I answer? She knows me too well. I can't chance it.

"Good. He's much nicer than I remember" is what I go with.

The forkful of eggs stops right in front of Grace's lips.

"What?"

"Yeah, super nice. We got a lot done. He's very professional."

Professional. Seriously, Shay?

Grace drops the fork and then presses her hand to my forehead.

I lean back and swat her away. "What are you doing?"

"Are you ill?"

"No, why?"

"You just gave Luca two compliments back-to-back."

"I … misjudged him?" I say and even I'm aware that it came out more as a question than a statement.

"What's going on?"

I groan and then drop my head into my hands.

I can't lie to her. I just said best friends are hard to find and I refuse to be a bad one.

"Luca only agreed to help me if I put in a good word with you so that he can ask you out, and I told him I would. I was desperate. Please don't hate me."

Grace grins. "I wondered how you got him to agree so easily, but outside of our career ethics, I have nothing in common with Luca."

"That's what I told him."

"And what did he say?"

"He said that you might have more in common if you knew more about him."

She grins and keeps eating.

"I know plenty, and although I think he'd be a catch for any girl, that girl is not me. But you should know that he asked me out a couple of nights ago and I turned him down."

"He did? You did?" I ask both questions so quickly, my voice squeaks.

Grace nods.

"Why did you turn him down?" It's a stupid question after the conversation we just had, but I blurt it out anyway.

"Because he's not my type. We just established that. Plus,

you're my best friend and your family hates him. It would be weird."

I frown.

"Don't let me stand in your way of dating someone."

Grace lets out a laugh.

"I'm not dating Luca."

"But if you wanted—"

"I don't."

I nod and then scrub my hands over my face and groan again.

"Why does desperation make you do stupid things?"

"Because if you did smart things, they wouldn't call it desperation."

I sit up and tap her nose.

"Exactly, but what do I tell him now? What if he backs out when I tell him I couldn't hold up my end of the deal? Or maybe I should just pretend that I'm still talking him up to you."

"Yes. That one. The Marina cannot suffer. Just say you're holding up your end of the deal, and every morning you can tell me one nice thing about him. You'd never be lying that way."

I chuckle. "Do you think I can come up with something daily?"

I ask it as a joke, but even I know that it'll be easy. Aside from what I will from here on out refer to as "the moment," he really was professional. He listened to me and what I wanted. He was very active in making a plan. I gave him crap about double-checking the measurements, but I loved that he did.

Hiring Luca was well overdue, but I won't be telling a single person that thought.

Especially not Luca.

"Yes, I do."

"Good. I'm glad one of us believes in me."

Grace winks and continues to finish her plate.

My hand drops to her arm.

"What if he asks you out again?"

My best friend shrugs. "I'll be polite, but the answer will still be no."

Her answer is so simple, and yet it makes me sad for Luca. He's going to get his hopes up and then nothing will come from it.

I shake all thoughts of a sad Luca from my mind and hold my head high.

Remodeling The Marina is back on track, and that is all I need to worry about right now.

As soon as breakfast is over, I head into town to pick up a few things for the bar and grab a coffee from Brooke's. I know I could make my own at The Marina, but it's just not the same.

With my bag of office supplies in hand, I pull open the door to B's Bakery, only to step back in a hurry as Linc Collins steps out.

"Oh, hey Shay. I didn't see you there."

He shows his friendly grin, and I return one.

"In a hurry?" I ask.

He nods. "I was actually going to come see you today. I talked to your mom on the phone this morning."

My stomach drops.

Already? The summer isn't over, and not to mention, what the heck time is it in Europe right now?

"Oh" is all I manage to get out. I look away from him because I've been told I have a face that gives away all my emotions, and right now, I don't want Linc to see that just knowing my parents have spoken to him could make me cry on the spot.

"Yeah." His toe taps. He has the decency to look guilty. "There wasn't anything set in stone, though. She just had a few questions on where to start if, you know, she decides to sell. I got the feeling she was still thinking it over."

I force a smile and nod. "Thanks, Linc."

"Anytime."

The door of the bakery swings open again, and this time it's Luca who steps out. He looks at me and then at Linc.

"What's going on?"

"Nothing," I say quickly.

"Just chatting," Linc adds.

"About what?" His demanding tone steals the show, and I find him watching me. His head tilts a little and his gaze locks on mine. "You good?"

I swallow, ready to tell him I'm fine, but then Miles walks out, followed by other locals.

An audience.

Great.

"That's none of your business," I snap at Luca and then look at Linc. "Have a good one."

I push past everyone and step into the bakery, letting out a breath when I see that Sadie and Brooke are the only two inside.

"What?" Brooke asks, standing taller as she takes me in.

Nothing major happened just now.

Just a simple reminder of the deadline I'm under and the fact that I hired the enemy to help me get it done, whom I have to hide from almost the entire town.

I blow out a breath.

"I think I'm in way over my head."

Sadie smiles and nods toward the front window.

"I think you might be right."

I follow her gaze to see Luca walking away, but his attention is on me as he passes the window.

As if I didn't have enough problems right now, my heart starts to race.

Just like it did all those years ago.

———

"I'M GOING to need to bring a trailer over tomorrow during the day."

I look up from where I've been working to find Luca standing in front of me with his hands on his hips. He's been working for the last hour, clearly working hard if the sweat marks on his chest have anything to say about it. In fact, he's sweating so much that his shirt sticks to his pecs just enough to outline them for me.

I swallow and then shake my head.

Hold it together, Shay.

Jesus.

"Not an option," I tell him and then go back to my computer.

Along with the renovations Luca is completing, I'm trying to plan other events in The Marina's backyard that line up with big events either at the lodge or with one of the many silly festivals our town holds each summer.

I call them silly only for the fact that it feels like our town will do anything to get everyone together. Like one big hangout. We just call them festivals, but still, my brother didn't do any of this when he was in charge, and then I'd skipped planning last summer to give this place a makeover, and now the new plan is to do everything at once.

Because, you know, I have so much free time these days. Between working at The Marina during the day and working with Luca at night, I'm busy.

"It's the only option," Luca counters, still talking about his trailer.

I let out a sigh.

"It's too risky. Someone might see you."

"You really don't think people will start to piece this together? I mean, suddenly this place looks brand-new and no one saw anyone working on it."

"No one is paying that close attention."

"This is Lovers. Everyone is paying close attention."

"Not to me."

"Especially to you."

My gaze snaps up.

"What does that mean?"

He shakes his head and goes back to where he's been measuring baseboards and marking them, then setting them in piles based on the marks. "It means that your family is well-known around here, Shay, and everyone knows they are currently overseas, so we are all watching out for you until the rest of the Parker pack returns."

He says each word with less and less excitement.

"Is that why you're so kind to me these days? To watch out for me?"

He grunts but doesn't say anything.

So I just roll my eyes as usual and get back to my computer.

Maybe five minutes pass. It was a glorious five minutes.

"What were you and Linc talking about this morning?"

I ignore him. I know, I know. It's not mature, but I need more work and less small talk.

"Shay."

"Luca."

"So you can hear me?"

"Of course I hear you. Everyone can always hear you."

"I'm going to let that slide on account of I think something is bothering you and you don't want to tell me."

I sit up and spin in my chair to face him. "If I were upset about something, why would you be the one that I come to?"

He shrugs.

"Because I'm a third party. It wouldn't have anything to do with me, so maybe I could help."

"Riiiiight. Because you're a true gentleman."

His gaze narrows before he takes a deep breath and gets back to work.

Again, maybe five minutes pass.

"You know," Luca starts, and I groan. "I actually am a gentleman, and that would be something nice for you to tell Grace."

I hold my pen in the air without looking at him.

"Noted."

The sigh that follows is so loud, I turn to tell him so but stop when I find him squatting, rearranging boards so that he can carry them to a new spot. He stands, the muscles in his legs pressing against his jeans and his flexing biceps so pronounced that I'm positive I'm about to see his sleeves rip apart.

He takes focused steps to the other side of the room.

"Can you come over here and move this box?" he asks over his shoulder.

"Okay," I say, moving quickly. Although I'm convinced that my body moved toward him before my mind deemed an answer.

I move the box then just stand there watching him.

Ogling him in a brightly lit room as he works.

Thinking about his legs and arms once more. Is the rest of his body as firm as they are? How much does that wood weigh? He carried it as if it were nothing.

A deep chuckle snaps me back to attention.

He caught me staring.

Shit.

I smirk and walk right by him.

"Sure. I didn't see anything," he mocks as I take my seat again.

I refuse to acknowledge him.

"I'm going to have one of the guys bring a trailer tomorrow," he says after I remain silent.

"Luca," I whine.

"I'll have them cover the company sign with something. Is there a special place he needs to park?"

I let out a breath. It's annoying how accommodating he's trying to be.

It makes it hard to dislike him.

"No, just wherever works is fine."

"Cool. So hey—" He pauses, waiting for me to look at him.

"What?"

He grips the back of his neck and pulls out his phone.

"I had questions earlier that I wanted to ask you, but I didn't want to call here and be obvious, so I think we should swap phone numbers."

If I didn't know any better, I'd say Luca is being shy.

It's adorable.

I freaking hate it.

I take his phone and add my number, then text myself.

"Is that all?"

He nods and quickly shakes his head. "I had an idea for the entrance to the restaurant."

"Luca," I warn, "I don't have time to make changes. We have a plan."

"I know, but I can still do it in the same timeline if you like it."

"No."

I don't need his ideas. I need mine.

"Just look at the picture."

"No."

"It's—"

"No."

"It's an arch!" he yells before I can cut him off again.

This time I keep my mouth shut.

"Do you remember that one summer forever ago when your mom kept saying everything in here was so boxy and you said there should be an arch? Well, I think we should do it."

"That was like fifteen years ago."

He shrugs. "Ever since you said it, I thought it would be cool."

He holds his phone up as if he's scared I might bite.

I take it and have to contain my glee as my eyes take in the photo. The arch is beautiful with built-in shelves on each side that are filled with different flowers and plants, giving it a slight greenhouse vibe.

"I even thought I could add the shelves if you like that look. The big windows would be perfect for it. It would have an earthy feel that I think would be great for when people come in off the water after a day in the sun. They still get that outdoorsy feeling, but the air conditioner would be highly enjoyable."

He lets out a laugh as he takes his phone back.

The look on my face makes his grin drop.

"Or you know, we could stick to the original plan. It's perfect for this place, too."

He turns to walk away, which is good because tears threaten my eyes.

Ever since I came back to Lovers, I wanted someone, anyone, to talk about The Marina the way I do. To see it the way I do. To love it the way I do, and just now, Luca did that.

I could see in the way he looked around the room as he spoke that he could see it. Heck, I could hear it in his voice.

I clear my throat.

"I want three shelves on each side instead of two," I say without looking at him.

Then I swipe away a tear that escapes.

Luca Asher, my number one enemy, just filled my heart with hope.

CHAPTER EIGHT

LUCA

It's almost been a week of me showing up at The Marina to work at night. I'm not convinced that this town hasn't caught on by now, but at the same time, not a single person has said a word to me, so maybe we're pulling this off after all.

What I'm not pulling off, however, is good sleep.

This new schedule has completely thrown me, and I need to find a new way to balance it out.

Soon.

Until then, just a little extra coffee, maybe a little extra protein as soon as I wake up, and I should be good as new.

I quickly get ready and head to work. A few hours in and I know that if I'm gonna struggle for the rest of the day, I need some comfort food, and that means a large ass coffee from B's Bakery and maybe even two sandwiches from Hudson's to keep on hand for when I'm hungry.

I park in front of the bakery and spot the line as soon as I reach the door.

Dammit. This is definitely a con of living in a small town.

As soon as I walk through the door, I spot Sadie as the second person from the cash register. So I shoot her a quick text with my order and then I take a seat at the table where her laptop is already set up.

Do I wish people knew I was helping at The Marina? Sure, yeah, but mainly because, even though I have a handful of projects happening right now, I just want to be at The Marina. If I could work there all day for eight hours instead of three stolen ones at night, I'd be so much further along and Shay could finally see some progress.

I can see in her eyes that she wants things to move faster, and I don't blame her. It's been a long process.

But we can't rush it if we want it done right.

I chuckle.

Could you imagine if I told her that? She'd flip. She'd probably have some comeback about how I'm not experienced enough or how she could hire someone else, and I'd tell her I'm well beyond experienced and that she loves that she hired me, and well, we'd just bicker like an old married couple for the night.

I wipe a hand over my face to swipe the grin away.

I don't think I should enjoy the way we banter as much as I do.

I lean back in my seat and wait for Sadie to join me, then I spot her walking toward me with two coffees, so I jump up to grab them for her.

Once we are sitting across from each other, she gives me a knowing look.

"Tired?" she asks.

I sip my coffee with a nod.

"Very."

"Late night?"

She looks down at her cup, but I still catch her lips tug up.

"You know, don't you?"

Her nose scrunches, and she nods. "But only because Shay told me about it."

"What? When?"

"At girls' … I ran into her here."

I narrow my gaze at my soon-to-be sister-in-law. She has the decency to look away.

"She just randomly blurted it out."

Sadie nods.

"No, she did not, Sadie Collins Future Asher."

That's the sentence that makes her cave.

"Fine, okay. She told me," Sadie leans in to whisper the rest of the sentence, "at girls' night."

I sit back as if she slapped me.

"Girls' night?" I repeat.

"Yes."

"You and Shay hang out enough to have a girls' night?"

"Yes."

This is news to me. Does Hudson know? He's mentioned Shay's name a time or two at Sunday breakfast, but now I'm starting to think he might know more than me.

"Who else goes to these nights?"

"Brooke, Grace, and Quinn."

"What?" I snap, drawing Brooke's attention from behind the counter, where she's talking to one of her employees.

"Stop, it's not a big deal."

"It's a huge deal."

Sadie shakes her head.

"It's not. Sometimes we just need to hang out with other girls and relax. It's therapeutic."

Therapeutic.

Nothing about that sounds therapeutic to me. What has Shay told them? If Grace is there and she knows, does she know Shay's half of the deal?

This does not look good for me.

"Do all the girls know about my working for Shay?"

She nods. "Maybe not Quinn. She's been busy with Miles."

"How often do you have these nights?"

"Twice a month at least, but weekly if we can."

"Twice a month or weekly?" I ask in disbelief. "What does Hudson do when you're there?"

Sadie shrugs. "I don't know. He hangs out and waits for me."

"He could call me."

"He could." She agrees and then grins. "Or you could have a boys' night."

"Boys' night."

"Yeah."

It sounds so weird and yet …

"That's not a half-bad idea. For tonight."

Especially since I now need to know what my brothers seem to know about me.

I grab my coffee, stick my hand in the air to wave good-bye, then I head out the front, turning for Hudson's. Lucky for me, Miles and Hudson are both here.

"Boys' night. Tonight. My house," I say and pull up a seat next to Miles.

"Can't. I'm busy with Quinn," he says and takes the to-go bag from Hudson.

I glance at Hudson.

"I know Sadie is busy already."

"I'll hang out," he says. "Just us?"

"Tell Linc and …" I glance round the room and spot Declan Young two seats down from my left. Declan grew up here, but then he left for college and started a tech company. I heard he got married and had a kid, but his wife left him and his daughter a year ago, so he moved back here to raise her.

Of course, I heard all of this through the rumor mill, so there is a high chance it's not true. I can find out at boys' night.

Oh, I'll recruit Dutton Richford, too.

"Declan," I say in a little louder tone.

He turns slowly to look at me. One brow raises as if to say, *you're bothering my alone time.*

"Luca."

His voice is a lot deeper than I remember. We were in the same grade, but I didn't spend a lot of time with him. He was too busy setting academic records at school while I was just trying to make it through the day before I could get outside and away from a desk. I vaguely remember Ruby complaining later when she hit junior high how much she hated hearing his name mentioned by all the teachers.

"You feel like coming to a boys' night tonight?"

"Nope."

"Come on, man. It's gonna be the first night of a tradition. You should come to my house. Be there."

"Yeah? You got a babysitter on hand for my daughter?"

His voice is laced with sarcasm, but I'm gonna pretend that it's not, because we *are* having boys' night and it needs to be more than just me and my brother and my brother's best friend.

Not to mention the fact that perhaps I could use a new friend who doesn't know my history when I need to vent a little.

"You moved next door to my dad, right? Lucky for you, Ruby is in town visiting."

Declan just chuckles.

"I bet Ruby would watch her. Have you talked since you moved back?" I add, just in case he didn't fully understand.

Declan glances between me and Hudson.

"Look, I don't wanna start any drama, but there is a 110 percent chance that your sister is never going to do favors for me."

I smirk.

Ruby must still hold a grudge for some reason. Typical Asher move.

"Write your number down on that coaster, and I'll see what I can do."

I'm aware that he doesn't sound too crazy about hanging out, but I'm going to invite him anyway. He's my age, and he needs people in this town on his side. And if the rumors are true, his daughter is the same age as my nephew and they will get along great.

Declan stares at me as he thinks about his choices, but eventually, he writes his phone number on the coaster, slides it across the bar top, and then leaves. I immediately start a group text with Hudson, Linc, Declan, Dutton, and Miles, because he gets to be a part of this whether he likes it or not.

LUCA

Tonight. My house. 6 p.m. Pizza. Beer.

Hudson's phone chirps, and he pulls it from his pocket. He reads it and then glances up at me.

"Were all the periods necessary?"

"Yes. I wanted to be straight to the point."

Hudson nods and gets back to work.

No argument or teasing or trying to come up with a reason he can't be there.

I smile just as a club sandwich appears.

And he knows my order now.

A year and a half ago, he'd have found any excuse not to spend time with me or Miles. Or anyone else for that matter.

Then the whole Sadie thing happened and he's the big brother I remember growing up.

I'm not going to cry or whatever, but until right now, I didn't realize how much I missed that side of him.

And Miles, he's keeping something from all of us, and I know it has to deal with Quinn, but considering my current situation and how I don't want anyone to ask me questions, I won't be hounding him anymore.

My phone buzzes.

LINC

Sounds good. I could use a night out.

LUCA

It's technically a night in.

LINC

Is this you changing my mind?

LUCA

Nope. See you tonight.

MILES

Heads-up for all who don't know by now,
but Luca is calling this boys' night.

DECLAN

I know. I just left Hudson's.

LUCA

And he's left his number. Hence why he's
replying to the text.

*Luca Asher has changed the name of the group to Boys'
Night Crew.*

DUTTON

Wrong number.

LUCA

It's not! Sorry, Dutton, I should have given
you a heads-up.

MILES

I didn't get one.

LUCA

Because you ran out of here too fast.

Declan Young has deleted the name of the group.

DECLAN

Can everyone just say yes so my phone
stops going off?

MILES

Raincheck. As you know.

DUTTON

Fine. Only because I need a drink.

LUCA

See you all tonight!

———

I'M NOT much of a host, but I think that six pizzas for six guys might have been overkill. Screw it, they can take a box as a parting gift when the night is over.

My front door opens, and Hudson walks in with a big smile. He lifts his hand, which has a twelve-pack of beer in it.

"I know you had some, but I wanted to contribute."

"Thanks. Pizza's in the kitchen."

He nods and heads that way just as I spot Linc, Declan, and Dutton hovering in my driveway.

"You boys coming in?" I ask, crossing my arms and leaning in the doorway.

Declan moves first.

"One beer and I'm leaving."

Fair enough.

"Thanks for the invite," Linc says and then walks in.

"Of course."

"I'm still not sure why I'm here," Dutton says, following right behind Linc.

Once everyone is inside, we gather in the kitchen.

Everyone is just looking at each other like it's weird to do this, but they each have a beer, so that's progress.

I open a box of pizza, grab a slice, and head for the living room.

"ESPN is on," I say. I hear various versions of *thank fuck,* then more boxes open and they all join me in the living room.

Dutton is on his second slice when he speaks up.

"What's the point of tonight? Do you have an announcement or something?"

I shake my head.

"Nope. Just wanted an excuse to hang out."

"He found out that Sadie and Grace have girls' nights," Hudson chimes in between bites.

Dutton chuckles, followed by Linc.

"Is that why your dad is watching the kids and not Ruby?" Declan asks.

"Shit, Ruby is going to girls' night now, too?"

"Why is girls' night a big deal?" This coming from Dutton.

"Because as of this morning, I was informed that they talk about us."

"Us. Who exactly is *us*?" Linc asks with finger quotes around the last word.

"You, me, everyone in this room."

"Who, Brooke?" Dutton sits up.

I shrug.

"Probably."

"They don't sit around and talk about us." Hudson laughs, but then his smile drops. "Do they?"

"It can't be that bad," Linc adds, his gaze clashing with a few of the guys. "Well, not for me. I'm friends with all of them."

"Must be nice." Dutton takes another sip of his beer.

"I'm no genius, but I'm guessing that you found out they

spoke about something that involves you specifically, so you needed a boys night for …”

Declan keeps his focus on me as he waits for me to finish his sentence.

“For the fact that we never hang out, and now, since we are all having a wonderful time, we will do this once a month.”

“Once a month?” Dutton practically gasps.

Hudson chuckles.

Linc nods in agreement.

And Declan, well, I don't know him well enough to know what his face means right now, but I don't think he’s totally against it.

My mouth opens to say more, but then my cell phone vibrates on the table. The moment I see Shay’s name pop up, I snatch that phone into my lap like a frog with a fly for dinner.

I can feel eyes on me, so I glance at Hudson.

His brow raises.

Shit. He saw it.

In my defense, I had no idea she was going to text me.

“Be right back,” I say and head for the kitchen.

SHAY: Do you still have that arch photo on your phone?
Luca: Yes.
Shay: Will you send it to me? I want to match some of those colors for this room.

I GRIN, typing out my response.

. . .

Luca: So she finally admits, in writing no less, that she liked my idea.

Shay: She just wants the picture.

Luca: Are you going to show the girls at girls' night? Be sure to tell them it was my idea.

THE LITTLE BUBBLES pop up and then disappear.

I chuckle, and a throat clears near me.

I glance up at Declan.

"Hey," I say and it comes out all high-pitched like I was caught breaking the rules somehow and don't want to get in trouble.

"Hi." He grins and grabs another beer.

He takes another slice of pizza with him to the living room.

I send Shay the picture with no further comment, and she doesn't supply one either.

When I get back to the living room, the guys are all laughing at something on the TV. Their chatter is on a roll now, too.

I sit back, taking in the view.

I don't know what I had in mind for this night, but I'll tell you what, just hanging out for the purpose of hanging out isn't half bad. Nowhere to be, no expectations, and no agenda.

It's nice.

A couple of hours later, I've got commitments for the next boys' night as they all walk out the door.

I'd say the night was a success.

I never got around to asking Hudson what he knows about my Shay situation. I'll have to save that for another day.

I glance out my front window. I can still see the glow of the streetlights.

I yawn a big yawn and let out a breath.

Then I sit on the couch and change the channel on the TV. I'll watch one episode of anything to keep me awake, and then I'll head to The Marina.

CHAPTER NINE

SHAY

Luca didn't show up last night. I was prepared to give him crap for mentioning my girls' night, but I can't do that if he isn't present.

I was half tempted to go search for him, but if anyone were to see me, it would have raised more questions than I need right now. I also thought about calling Grace to have her go check it out, but that seemed a bit too stalkerish for my liking.

So I just sat and stewed all night long.

I know I can be a lot to handle sometimes, but am I really so bad that I ran another contractor off?

I close the cash register drawer and hand the two customers in front of me their change.

Maybe I should open an ice-only shop. That seems to be the moneymaker these days. Then again, if I had a full dining room, maybe people would stick around to eat.

As soon as I'm alone again, sit at the bar top and open my

computer. With the progress Luca and I made after just a handful of nights, I may have gotten a little excited and started ordering the decor I wanted. I gave myself a specific budget for it, and I can't wait to start putting this place together again. I really do think the private areas in the dining section will be great for bigger parties, and I want each one to have a theme.

Well, I hope they get to have a theme anyway. If Luca doesn't come back, I'm screwed. That's it. I can't afford to waste more time looking for someone new.

I groan to no one.

I could always start watching YouTube videos and learn how to build a wall myself. I bet Grace would help me if I absolutely needed her.

With another deep breath, I scrub my hands over my face.

I can't give up.

I've come too far.

Still, I feel like there is so much against me right now. I'm the only one who sees what this place could be again and being the only one who believes in myself is exhausting. Luca was starting to make me feel like I wasn't alone in this anymore, but so much for that.

As if the universe wants to remind me of this, my phone rings with my brother's face appearing on the screen.

"Leo, I thought you only called me at night when you couldn't sleep?"

"Yeah, well, I thought I'd surprise you with a call during the day when you might be more willing to talk."

"I'm always willing to talk."

I don't like the direction his conversation is headed.

"Mom and Dad are talking about reaching out to Linc again when they get back."

"What?" I practically yell into the phone as I stand and start to pace.

Again. One call to him is one thing, but multiple?

Do I even still have a chance?

"The summer isn't over yet."

"No, but they must have someone keeping an eye on you, because word is, your contractor bailed and now the renovations are halted. Selling that place is going to be even harder now that it's half finished."

"It's … I have a new contractor, and we just got started this week. Let the word get around about that."

But not too much.

Shit.

"Who is it?"

My frustration is so heavy right now that a part of me almost blurts out that it's Luca, but the other half of me knows admitting that would be more fuel to their current decision.

"Another out-of-state guy," I say instead.

Defeat runs through my entire body quickly.

I'm a grown woman and shouldn't need to lie, but until this place is legally in my name, I can't afford to tell them the truth.

"All right, well, I'll pass the message on. I can't promise it will change their minds though."

"No, but maybe they'll appreciate how proactive I'm being."

Just then, two guys who look to be in their twenties walk in through the back door. Both are in cutoff shirts, board shorts, and flip-flops. Sure, they look lake ready, but from the way they walk and the way they look at me, I know they aren't locals. I didn't even notice them pull up, but they are staring at me as if my lack of greeting is insulting. Which, to be fair, is not the image I want this place to have.

"I have to go. Give everyone my love," I tell Leo quickly and hang up.

"Hi, there. What can I do for you?" I ask, moving around to the employee side of the bar top.

The man with dark hair grins as I speak, not answering my question, but he does stop at the bar on the other side of me. He leans on his forearms, his eyes on me the entire time.

Okay, creeper.

I glance at his buddy, who just chuckles and heads for the ice cooler. He pulls out two small bags. Since guy number one isn't going to speak, I ring them up.

"Is that all?"

Guy number one takes a five from his back pocket and hands it to me. I reach for it, but he doesn't let go.

"And your phone number," he says with a wink.

Oh, for fuck's sake. Can't a girl just go to work and that be that?

"Sorry, not today."

"So if I come back tomorrow?"

I hand him back his change.

"It'll be a no then, too. Have a good day, and come back if you need anything else."

I move as if I'm busier than ever and have other places to be, but this one is relentless.

"Oh, come on. What does a guy gotta do to get your number?"

Shit.

I thought I'd be able to walk out of the room before we got to this point, but it seems I wasn't fast enough.

The Marina has been through a lot over the years, and one might think I have a long list of things that bother or annoy me, but despite the troubles in the past, the only thing I can't stand about this place is the number of men who come in here and think a small conversation ends with them getting my number.

It's as if they don't understand that this is my job—it helps me to be kind to all customers.

It by no means should be interpreted that I'm flirting.

Alas, here we are.

I turn slowly to find guy number one's eyes on my ass.

He looks up and licks his lip, then nods.

"You gonna give it to me or what?"

Oh, hell no.

"Dude"—his friend swats his shoulder—"Let's go. This place is like half finished, and I feel like I'm breathing in sawdust just standing here."

Oh, sure, add salt to the wound of already being insulted by the fact that this man in front of me thinks he stands a chance. Now I have to be reminded that Luca didn't show up last night.

"Let me get this hottie's number first."

There is no way in hell I'm giving this man my number. "You know," I start, but then the main door opens and Luca strides in as if being here in broad daylight is the most normal thing in the world.

This day just keeps getting better and better.

How dare he show up here right now.

"Your number. Come on."

I don't know who I dislike more right now, but screw both of these men.

My lips part to tell the guy in front of me to bug off—fuck off might be a little harsh for a customer—but then a better idea forms.

"Let me write it down," I tell him.

I scribble out a number I've known by heart for as long as I can remember and say, "It's best if you text me. And to be honest, I need details. If you want to take me out, I need to know when, where, for how long, and what the ending kiss could be like. Everything. In a text, please."

I hand him the number and wink.

His smile is so big, I almost feel bad.

"Easy," he says with a smirk and then walks off.

Sure was.

Feeling slightly immature but also pretty damn good about the choice I just made, I turn for the dining area, which is blocked off by construction plastic.

I whip the plastic back and waste no time scowling at Luca as he follows me.

Quietly, I snap, "What are you doing here? Are you insane?"

He doesn't even bother looking over his shoulder as he measures the longest wall.

"I wanted to double-check this measurement. I think we could put in another window here, and it would bring in more natural light, giving a nice view of the east side of the lake."

"Maybe if you would have showed up last night, you could have gotten them hung. Now go. I told you I didn't want you here during the day."

"Hey, I'm sorry about last night, okay. I got caught up, then I fell asleep. Trust me. I'm not happy about it either."

"Sure. Whatever. This is my job, Luca, and if you can't hold up your end of the deal, then I won't either."

He huffs.

"What have you told Grace by now anyway? You know, when you're at girls' night."

I yank the tape measure from his hand and point a hard finger at him. Ignoring his jab about girls' night, I say, "Up until last night, I said you were a hard worker. I'll probably say something else now."

"I am, and shit, Shay, really? No woman is going to fall for a man because of his hard-working traits. What if she portrays that as I'm too invested in my job to be in a relationship or something?"

I'm too stunned to even have a witty comeback.

Being a hard worker is a great trait. Having a partner who is motivated to do their best is sexy, but yeah, like hell I'm going to share that with him.

"Whatever. Like I said, if you don't hold up your end of the deal, I won't either."

"I'll work double time tonight to make up for it." His head hangs low as he speaks. He appears remorseful, but I'm too angry to care right now.

"Nope."

"What? You're firing me?"

"Nope. It just so happens that you get two nights off now, because I have a new date tonight and won't be here. Therefore, you do not need to be here."

The words are out of my mouth before I can think. I can't afford not to get things done two nights in a row.

Dammit, brain. Just let him win once in a while if it means you get this marina done.

He scoffs. "A date. With who?"

"That's none of your business."

"It's a little my business since you're canceling tonight for this date."

I roll my eyes. "You don't know him."

"Why not?"

"He lives in Wind Valley, and that's where the date is."

Ha. Take that one, Luca Asher.

Now, not only will I not have to think of a name, I won't even have to go out. And another plus—I can hide in my house all night.

A night off.

Hmm, I really nailed this one. This is better than me giving that guy Luca's number.

"You're going on a date in town that's two hours away, and you've never met the guy before?"

His head tilts as his eyes bore into mine. He crosses his arms as he waits for my answer.

I nonchalantly let out a breath at his possessive stance.

It's not hot.

It's not.

It's NOT!

"It's … not a first date," I say slowly, and I'm not even convinced by my own words.

We stand there, glaring at each other, a clear battle of who is going to cave first. As soon as Luca opens his mouth, I smile in victory.

Until I hear what comes out next.

"I'll drive you."

"What? No way."

"Yes, way."

"No," I say, this time with a small stomp of my foot.

"You're not going to win this one. You might hate me—hell, your whole family does—but that doesn't change the fact that letting you go meet a guy you've never met before does not sit well with me. You won't even know I'm there."

"Doubtful."

I take a deep breath. I want to keep arguing, but I can see in his eyes that this is something he isn't going to budge on

It's sweet in a way.

In its own possessive way.

Kind of … hot, too.

Oh hell, listen to me.

Too many emotions are running through me right now, because not only do I agree with his thought process on going alone to a date that doesn't exist, but his comment about my family hits home.

We've let one bad choice dictate our opinion of him since, and here he is, being considerate of them.

Clearly, the Luca from back then and the Luca now are not the same person. Well, they're a little the same but still different.

"What time is your date?" he asks, ready to move on with the subject.

Against my better judgment, I say, "It's at 5."

"In three hours. Jesus, Shay. I'll be back in an hour to pick you up."

I give him a nod that says I can't wait and then I tack on a thumb's-up.

As soon as he's out the door, I pull my phone from my back pocket and dial Grace's number.

"Hey, babe, what's up?"

"Can you meet me at my house?"

"Oh, wow, now?"

"Yes, it's urgent."

"How urgent?"

"Like I just told Luca that I had a date with a stranger in Wind Valley tonight and then he demanded that he drive me to make sure I stay safe urgent."

"Well, that doesn't sound too bad. It's sort of sweet, really."

"Yes, it's wonderful. He's a true gentleman. Blah, blah, blah. But there is one problem."

"Okay?"

"I made the date up, and he's picking me up in an hour."

"Oh."

"Yeah, oh. Can you meet me?"

"I'm walking out the door now."

"Perfect. Thank you."

We end the call, and I check in with my small staff to let them know I'm leaving early tonight. Then I rush home to get ready for the date I don't have.

———

"You're sure you tried everyone you know in Wind Valley?"

I'm just adding matching gold earrings to my statement necklace as I speed walk through my kitchen to look out the front window.

"I swear, I tried them all."

"Ugh. Okay This is on me. This is what I get for lying."

"It could be fun if you let it. I mean, tell him you're going somewhere near that shop with the glass bookshelves. You like the coffee there, and you could sit in one of those big fluffy chairs and read for an hour, then say the date ended early and meet back up with Luca."

I pause and look at my best friend. My genius best friend.

"I'm definitely doing that," I tell her and then look out the window again.

"Why do you keep looking outside?"

"Because if any of my neighbors see Luca pick me up, I'll never hear the end of it. I'm just making sure no one is outside."

"Okay," Grace laughs. "By the way, I have to say, for a not real date, you look hot tonight."

"Thank you."

I glance in the hallway mirror and run my fingers through my loose curls. Then I take in my burgundy V-neck top that has flowy sleeves and cinches at the waist. It's a short dressy top that stops just above the waist of my dark high-waisted jeans. There are holes in them, but not too many, and the strappy nude heels I added give me the perfect cute casual look. Or in Grace's terms, hot look.

"Luca is going to flip when he sees you."

"What does that mean? I didn't dress up for him."

"No, but I haven't seen you this dressed up in a while, and my guess is that neither has he. In fact, this very well may be the first time he sees the real grown-up Shay Parker."

"He knows I'm grown up."

"Yeah, in cutoff shorts and a tank top all day every day."

"That's not—shit, he's here. Look at him all dreamy or something so that he knows I'm talking him up."

"I'm not doing that." Grace laughs. "I won't lead him on."

Ugh. She's right. Why does my brain short circuit and take me back a year whenever Luca is involved?

Why can't I just be normal around him?

I rush back to my bedroom to get my purse, then dip into the bathroom once more to add one last spritz of perfume. When I come out to the living room, Grace is opening the door to reveal Luca.

Like me, he's showered and changed since earlier.

His hair is styled, and I'm pretty sure there is a little bit of gel in it. His shirt is clean, a simple dark green with sleeves that hug his biceps, and his jeans, held up by a dark tan belt, hang just perfectly off his hips. His shoes match the belt, and before I can even think of what to say, the smell of sandalwood fills the room.

Luca cleans up nicely.

Grace clears her throat. My gaze flashes to hers, and she presses her lips together.

"So, you two have fun tonight."

Luca is staring at me, but when we make eye contact, it must break whatever trance he was in, because he, too, clears his throat.

"It's not a date. Not for us. Not for me. But I'm open to dating. In general. Not Shay. But tonight isn't a date. I mean, she has one. I'm just … driving."

Luca sighs in defeat, and I hate to admit it, but rambling Luca is a tiny bit adorable.

"Noted." Grace grins and pats his shoulder before waving goodbye.

Since we have a deal where my part is to set him up with Grace, I expect to watch him take in her every move as she walks away or fawn over her for a moment, but he doesn't. Instead, he looks back at me.

"Um…" He clears his throat again. "Is that what you're wearing?"

"Yes." I put a hand on my hip, ready for him to pull some macho move and tell me to change. "Why?"

My tone must wake him up, because he glares at me.

"This guy better not be a douche, Shay."

"He's not."

"I'm serious."

"So am I," I say walking toward him then pushing him out the door so we can get this over with. I glance around to be sure there isn't an audience. When I think it's good, I speed walk to his truck.

"I'm not kidding, Shay. I don't want to get into a fight tonight."

That stops me.

"Why would you get in a fight tonight?"

"Don't play dumb," he says and opens the passenger door for me.

"I'm not." I climb in and watch him walk around the hood. As soon as he opens his door, I ask, "Why would you get in a fight tonight?"

He shakes his head and starts the car.

"Because I'm not an idiot or blind. If I were the guy meeting you for this date and you walked in looking the way you do right now, let's just say I wouldn't be about to let another man even set his eyes on you. You'd be mine and mine only. So yeah, this guy better not be a douche."

"Oh" is all I say before we are suddenly turning onto Main Street.

I duck down so fast that Luca flinches.

"What the fuck are you doing?"

"I don't want anyone to see me with you," I say quickly and then look away from his face.

Hell, I have to.

What Luca just said … wow.

Possessive Luca. I like it.

CHAPTER TEN

LUCA

I haven't punched anyone since my junior year of high school when Barney Evens started a cheap rumor about my little sister Ruby, but I'm pretty sure it's like riding a bike.

It'll all come back to me when the moment arises.

But fuck, I hope it doesn't. Actually, I'm sort of hoping that her date stands her up.

Fuck. I feel shitty for thinking that way, but wow.

I steal another glance at Shay as we pull into Wind Valley.

Shay's always been pretty, and I've noticed as her curves have made themselves more visible over the years, but I always knew how to leave it at that, just looking. Maybe a sexual innuendo in a conversation here and there, but nothing serious.

Even if I wanted to, I wouldn't stand a chance in her eyes, and her family's distaste for me would make it impossible, but tonight, when I stepped into her living room, it was like I was seeing a side of Shay I'm not supposed to see. The side that wants to tempt me to change our entire relationship.

I'm not just saying she looks hot. Shay looks absolutely stunning tonight. Gorgeous isn't even a good enough word for her. She looks … like I never want to look away.

Fuck.

FUCK.

"So where am I dropping you off?"

I mean for the question to be considerate, but I'm pretty sure I growled by the last word. And I don't growl for anyone. Ever.

"Um, it's a bar called The Black Alcove."

She's looking at her phone as if she needs to be reminded where to go.

"Your date is at a bar?" Even my voice is unimpressed.

"Yep. It's newly remodeled with a new menu and music for everyone."

What the … is she reading that right from her phone?

I pull into a spot out front and slowly look around. There aren't any loiterers, so if her date is here, he wasn't man enough to wait outside for her. I should walk her in and prove a point to this jackass.

I unlock my seat belt at the same time as Shay.

"What are you doing?" The panic in her voice makes me pause.

"Walking you to the door."

"I don't need you to walk me to the door."

"Well, I don't see your date waiting for you, and I'm not just going to let you go in alone. What if he stands you up and then you spend the night alone? Because let's be real here, you wouldn't tell me if he did."

The briefest smile touches her lips, but she catches herself and rolls her eyes.

"I'll call you if he doesn't show."

"Swear it."

"I swear."

Another eye roll.

I can't place it. I really can't, but I do not like this right now. I'm half tempted to reach for her, pull her back into the truck, and beg her to stay with me. I'll take her somewhere. Anywhere she wants.

This is new for me when it comes to her.

"I mean it, Shay. Swear that you'll call me."

"Oh god. Yes, daddy, I swear I'll call you if I need you to save me."

Her voice is laced with sarcasm, but I... just ... can't right now.

I close my eyes for a split second and pinch the bridge of my nose. "Get out of the fucking truck."

Her laughter is the last thing I hear before she closes the door.

She even sticks her tongue out at me as she crosses in front of the truck.

And then she smiles. It's a genuine, pure Shay Parker smile, and I swear my heart skips a beat.

I sit in my truck as I wait for Shay to walk into the bar. My actions are twofold. I want her to get inside safely, but I also can't stop looking at her.

Jesus.

I've never felt more like a creep than I do right now.

I'd be lying if I said I never thought of her as more than my friend's sister more than once growing up, but that was that. I never shared those thoughts with anyone and then when my friendship with her brother fell apart, I didn't see the point in ever letting those thoughts consume me again. But right now, hell, it's going to be hard not to forget her now.

The door to the bar closes, so I lean my head back and take a breath.

It's not just her body that gets under my skin.

It's her wit. The way she can get me worked up because her mind is quick like mine. I love it. The way she keeps up in conversation with me. The way she tries, and fails, to hide her smile when I say something she likes. The way she taps her toe behind her right before she gives me a compliment while she's looking at my work.

I love that she knows what she wants with The Marina and her life. I love that she's focused.

I love a lot of her fire and passion in life, and holy fuck.

I think I'm crushing on Shay.

Shit.

My eyes spring open as this revelation takes over.

This is bad.

So, so bad.

What should I do?

Nothing. Of course. That would be a disaster. Her family would kill me.

The idea of us is impossible. It always has been.

Even knowing this, I have to let out a breath, because now that I'm aware of these feelings, the obstacles to why we don't make sense seem irrelevant.

I back out of my parking spot, resisting the urge to go inside to make sure her date isn't a creep.

I pop into one of the hardware stores a few blocks over for a few things then return to the bar, finding the first open parking spot. It's in front of a bookstore, but I'm headed to the coffee shop, Loves a Brewing, that's connected to the book-store. If I'm going to have to wait for Shay and remind myself that I can't ruin her date over something I just realized, I need caffeine. Plus, who knows how late this could go? I'm driving us back and need to stay awake.

Warm air brushes my skin as I step inside. The place is vacant. I'm not sure what time they close, but I assume it's soon.

"Hi," a woman greets me. "What can I get you?"

"Just a black coffee."

She makes it quickly, and I pay then move to the middle of the store that connects to the bookstore.

I'm not the biggest reader in my family. That title now belongs to Sadie, but there is just something about being in a bookstore that I like.

I look up to the signs over each aisle, looking for the—

"Oh, that's one of my favorites," a woman's voice says from a few rows over.

It's familiar. Too familiar, and I stop what I'm doing.

I shouldn't eavesdrop, but what the heck?

As if I'm now some kind of spy, I tiptoe and move as stealthily as I can toward the voice, which is now giving more book recommendations to someone.

When I'm pretty sure she's just one row over, I peek slowly, and sure as hell, there's Shay sitting in a corner set up with a round cozy pink chair that looks like it should be on someone's front porch given the way it hangs from the ceiling and end tables for the coffee lovers to sit and read. She's got a coffee and a book as she tucks one leg under the other and laughs at something the other woman has said. My eavesdropping must have frozen me the moment I spotted Shay, because I have no idea what was so freaking funny.

I narrow my gaze, ready to step up to her and demand she explain herself. She swore she'd call me if her date didn't show.

But then I stop.

She's smiling and laughing and she looks … happy. She looks the least stressed or sad I've seen her in weeks.

As much as I want to know the truth right now, I can't take this from her.

Hell, listen to me. My brain clicks in that I like her, and now all of a sudden I'm letting her just … how bad do I have it?

I step back to where she can't see me and turn to let myself out of the store.

As I make my way back to my truck, all I can think is *did she even have a date tonight?*

—————

I CAN'T KEEP the smile off my face as I watch Shay step out of the bar where she was having her so-called date.

Ha.

If it weren't for the fact that I saw her in the bookstore, the to-go container in her hand would be pretty convincing.

Hell, up until I saw her, I had no reason to doubt that she wasn't on a real date. What really boggles me is why she lied. I have a hunch, of course, but I'm starting to wonder if I can't get her to crack and tell me the truth.

Our eyes meet through the front window of my truck, and she gives me a tight-lipped smile before she looks away.

She's not thrilled that I invited myself to drive her to Wind Valley, and I have to look away to keep myself from laughing.

Now I know why.

I get out and meet her at her door.

"Oh, really, Luca. I can get in a truck on my own."

"I know, but a good date would get the door for you, and since he seems to be lacking, I guess I'll have to do it."

She climbs in, zero response to my comment, and I can't help it. I smile the entire way back to my side and keep on smiling when I get in.

"Hi," I say and then lean back.

"Hi," she says with a little wrinkle between her eyes as she looks at me. "What's with the creeper grin?"

"Nothing."

I do my best to control it, but I just can't stop smiling at her.

"Are we going?" she asks and clicks her seat belt into place.

"Sure, yeah."

Her gaze narrows as she looks at me one more time before staring straight out the window.

"Let's go then."

Now, there are two ways I can go about this. One, pretend that she was on a date the way she's doing and just move on with my night, or two, see how far she's willing to take this lie.

This situation right here is the most exciting one I've been in in a while, so I have to go with the latter.

Plus, you know, this whole newfound crush thing makes me suspicious as hell.

Especially because, despite not knowing what is

happening right now, whatever she's pulling makes me even more interested in her.

How twisted am I?

"The truck isn't moving," she states and points at the road.

"How was your date?" I cross my arms.

Seems I don't have any plans to start driving. I'm just going by the seat of my pants here.

"Good. Let's go."

"Where?"

"Home," she says slowly. "Where else would we go?"

"I don't know. I might need a coffee for the drive back."

"Coffee. Now?"

"Yeah. Don't you want one?"

"No."

"A book, then, maybe."

I bite my lip to keep from bursting into laughter.

"Nope. I'm good."

"I bet you are," I say and chuckle. I'd intended to keep that thought to myself, but it seems my mouth had other plans.

"What's wrong with you? Did you drink while I was eating dinner?"

"Did you?"

"Did I do what?"

"Eat dinner?"

"Oh my god. Give me the keys. You are not driving us back to Lovers."

She unbuckles her seat belt and reaches over to press the truck's start button, but I swat her hand away.

"I'll drive. You just tell me all about your date."

"I don't know if I trust your driving right now, Luca."

"Oh, you don't know if you trust me?" I finally pull onto

the road once she is sitting back in her seat, clicking her belt back into place.

"You're being so weird right now." She turns her attention to the phone in her hands and starts typing. I can see she's texting someone.

"Are you texting your date?"

"Yep. I'm telling him to come rescue me because my ride is clearly unstable."

"Should I pull over?"

"No."

"Are you sure?"

"Luca!"

"What?" I ask with a chuckle and then sigh. Fine. I'll cool it.

Instead of replying, she just laughs. "Please swear to me that you can drive right now."

I nod. "I'm fine, Shay."

"Promise."

"I promise."

At that she groans.

"What now?"

"Nothing."

"It's something."

"It's nothing."

"Tell me."

"Tell me why you're acting strange," she argues back.

I nod slowly.

"I'll tell you when I drop you off."

She laughs again, only this time it's not sarcastic. She pulls her phone out, and a quick glance shows her playing on social media. "You're so weird."

I grin because, just like her laugh, there is nothing sarcastic in her tone.

So what if she called me weird.

I can be weird, especially if it earns me a smile like the one she has now.

Traffic is basically nonexistent on the way home, so we make it in record time. The only light left is that of the neighborhood streetlights.

I pull up in front of her house and put the truck in park, glancing to her side. Shay fell asleep about ten minutes ago.

I don't want to read too much into it, but the fact that she is comfortable enough to relax this way around me says a lot.

Like maybe she doesn't dislike me as much as she lets on.

I'm not sure what to do with that information.

I take one more moment to study her.

Hudson told me once that when he finally realized his feelings for Sadie, they hit hard and fast.

Maybe it's an Asher trait. Right now, the last thing I want to do is wake Shay up so she can go inside and I can go home.

This is crazy.

I let out a breath of a laugh and then reach for her.

Do I shake her? Tap her thigh? Poke her shoulder?

What's the protocol here?

I clear my throat.

Then I clear it louder.

And then I cough.

Shay startles and sits up.

"Oh, we're here."

"Yep."

I climb out and walk around to her side.

When I pull the door open, she rolls her sleepy eyes at me.

I like it.

Damn it.

"One of these days, you'll listen and stop opening my door for me."

"Unlikely."

I follow her to the door, and as soon as we reach it she shoves me back.

"Go away. I can open my own door."

"I know." Grinning like a fool, I rest a palm to the door frame as she turns the handle, and then I lean in. "But then I wouldn't get to see your face when I tell you that I hope you had a great time with your coffee and books in Wind Valley. I know I did."

She sucks in a breath, and my gaze flashes to her pink lips as they part.

Then my heart pounds and my brain screams, *kiss her!*

I lean in, and I swear her eyes close as if she's going to let me do it, as if she wants it, too, but then I feel the heat of her hands on my chest as she pushes me again.

"Gah! You're the worst."

She ducks inside and slams the door in my face.

I walk back to my truck with my head hung low.

I'm so fucked.

CHAPTER ELEVEN

SHAY

If you could actually die of embarrassment, I would have dropped dead on my front porch last night in front of Luca.

It's one thing to lie about having a date, but to lie to someone who drove you to another town, caught you on your not date, then held onto that secret just to reveal he knew the truth hours later is … I'm dead. How do I go about this now? He's going to have the upper hand in our teasing, and I can't have that.

I walk a little faster as I near Sips and Stories, Sadie's bookstore. I texted her, Grace, and Brooke first thing this morning for an emergency girls' night, but because they all have lives, we are having an impromptu lunch hour meetup in the sports romance section.

I walk in the door, glancing to the side of the store that opens up to Hudson's Bar. The lunch rush hasn't hit yet, so I quickly make my way to the aisle I need. All of the girls are waiting for me.

"There she is." Sadie beams.

"Good. I want to know what happened last night." Grace grins.

"What was last night?' Brooke asks.

"Shhh." I wave a hand for them to keep their voices down, and then I peek out of the aisle.

We're alone.

Good.

"Last night," I begin in a whisper, "I made up a fake date, and Luca drove me all the way to Wind Valley for it, only for him to see me at the bookstore, not on a date."

Grace cracks up while Brooke and Sadie just smile.

"So, I feel as if I'm missing some details," Sadie says.

I fill them in on how it all came to be then huff.

"And he knew the entire drive home and waited until he walked me to the door to tell me."

"Oh, he walked you to the door? That's sweet," Brooke swoons.

"Not sweet. Annoying."

The girls all share a glance, but I'm too worked up over my situation to analyze it right now. Because basically, I don't need to analyze what they are thinking. I know it.

I like Luca.

They aren't completely wrong, but saying it in my head versus admitting it out loud are two completely different things.

"So now, when he comes over tonight—"

"Ladies," a deep voice comes from behind us.

Sadie brushes past me to wrap her arms around Hudson's neck and pull him in for a kiss.

"You're overreacting," Grace whispers after Brooke

excuses herself to go back to the bakery. Sadie is fully smitten by her fiancé now, so it's just me and Grace.

"Am I?"

"It's just Luca. You don't care what he thinks anyway."

She grabs a book and reads the back blurb while I let her words sink in.

I actually do.

Care.

I groan.

"At the same time, what if you just act normal around him? No comebacks, no quick anything. Just plain old kind Shay. As if you were hanging out with me."

"I can't do that," I admit on a sigh.

Grace checks her watch. "I have to get back to the lodge. Walk with me?"

I nod, and we tell Sadie goodbye.

That impromptu girls' meetup wasn't any help. Other than that, I did get to tell someone my problem, and that alone is helpful.

As soon as we step out the door, Luca and Miles are walking up to the bar. Luca's gaze snaps to mine instantly.

I think Grace and Miles exchange pleasantries, but I can't be sure. I'm too focused on the way Luca's T-shirt hugs his chest.

His eyes slowly move from my face, down my body, and back up.

My body buzzes as if he were right in front of me, touching me, slowly running his hand up my arm until he threads his hand through my hair and tilts my chin, letting his lips hover over my mouth as if he were going to kiss me.

The way I thought he was going to last night when he walked me to my door.

I don't say anything, and neither does he. He simply nods with a smirk on his face. Then he looks at Grace, and my heart sinks.

It shouldn't do that.

Not when I'm supposed to be annoyed at him over last night.

Gosh, this whole thing is messed up, and I'm tired of it taking all my brain power.

I just don't know what to think about it.

The Marina should be my focus, not Luca.

Turns out, I don't have to worry too much about it right now. Luca and his brother disappear into the bar.

"Wow," Grace says quietly beside me.

"What?" I fall into step with her.

"You and Luca not talking when you saw each other was weird."

I give her a side-eye.

"Do you like him?"

"What?" I ask and almost trip.

"Do you like Luca?"

"No."

"It's okay if you do. I've made it clear I'm not into him that way."

"I don't, though."

My immediate answer is all too telling.

"Okay, so then, what's your plan for tonight?"

"I don't know. We need to go look at the cabins. My last guy never got to them, and I'd like to get the minor stuff fixed before winter so that I can still rent them out. We can do more renovations later, and I—"

"I meant with Luca."

"Oh." I think it over for a moment. "I'm not sure yet."

"Well" —she bumps my shoulder as we pause at the corner of the street where she will go left and I'll go right to work—"maybe don't do anything. See what happens. If he didn't say anything just now, maybe he won't at all. I know you two have that thing you do, but I don't think he'd ever say anything to intentionally embarrass you."

"Luca? Not say anything? That's wishful thinking."

But really, she might be right.

"Just be nice. Maybe you two could be friends."

Friends.

With Luca.

I let out a sigh.

I could never be just friends with Luca.

My immature response to everything he says or does is how I keep him in the spot we are in. How I keep him from getting too close and vice versa. If it weren't for the way we are together, I'd have forgiven him a long time ago.

Any other spot, including so-called friends, sounds complicated.

I don't want anything in my life to be complicated.

I nod at my best friend. "I'll think about it." And then I wave goodbye.

Want it or not, it's what I have.

———

I'VE CHOSEN to go with the path of not speaking to Luca tonight.

Mature, I know. Let's just say that this summer isn't filled with my best moments. I guess that saying about how desperate people make bad decisions is more accurate than I thought.

But also, I feel like not speaking and saying something snarky could actually be the mature way to go. We are choosing not to bicker. It's new for us.

Yeah, I'm going with that.

Has it crossed my mind that perhaps because he's also unusually quiet, something is bothering Luca? Yes, but I'm not going to ask him about it and chance him bringing up my not date from yesterday.

Tonight is actually not a bad night, so I'm not going to jinx it. We have music playing to fill the silence. Every now and then I hear Luca sing along, and I absolutely do not think it's cute that he knows every word to a Swifty song.

I'm sorting through the paint swatches I picked for each room so that I can get an order together. Luca is proficient, and even though we are currently ignoring each other, the fact that I can be doing this stuff instead of watching his every move is refreshing.

Maybe this is what it's like to just be normal.

I'll be sure to tell Grace that I took her advice.

And yet, when Luca's phone vibrates against the table, for what feels like the hundredth time in ten minutes, I'm ready to snap.

"Oh my god, does your phone ever stop going off?"

He groans, sits back on his heels, and grabs it from the table.

His face wrinkles as he reads whatever is on the phone. I'd ask what's wrong, but I don't really care. I care about the work we're getting done tonight.

Well, that's what I tell myself anyway.

"I just love that someone else on your phone is more important than what I'm paying you to do right now."

Luca tosses his phone onto a stack of boards and goes back to work. He's cutting the boards to make the arch. He said he'd have it done before he left tonight.

Not thirty seconds later, his phone is vibrating again.

"I'm going to smash that thing with my hammer."

"Chill, okay. It's a wrong number issue, and this guy clearly doesn't get the hint. Actually, you'd love this."

He tosses me his phone, and I start to read.

UNKNOWN

Come on, baby. Stop acting like you didn't want me to text you these things. Do you want more details? You said you love detail. After I kiss you goodnight, I'll—

I stop reading instantly and turn to face the opposite wall as I do my best to compose myself, but it's hard. My lips instantly spread into a smile and my eyes sting with happy tears.

This. Is. Awesome.

I forgot I'd given that guy Luca's number.

This is total karma for last night.

I take a breath, fan my eyes for a moment, then spin to hand him back his phone.

I'm not expecting Luca to be right behind me when I turn around, and I'm not expecting him to be looking at me as if he can read my mind either.

"Here," I say, swallowing the lump in my throat and keeping my expression as neutral as I can.

"You don't think it's funny?"

I shrug and do a non-committal head shake.

"Not even a little?"

"Poor guy" is all I say.

Luca nods slowly. "How do you know it's a guy? Why are your eyes glistening?"

"Excuse me?"

"You heard me. They are shining like someone who was laughing but had to do it quietly, so her eyes started shining as she held it in."

To that I laugh.

"You're nuts."

"What did you do?"

"Me?" I place a hand on my heart. "Why is this suddenly a thing where I did something?"

"Because my life was smooth sailing until you popped back into it."

Funny. I feel the exact same way.

"I doubt it was."

"Shay, did you give someone my number?"

I shake my head.

How does he know this? We've only been around each other a couple of weeks, and now he just knows me.

I don't accept that.

"Shay."

"No."

"Shay," he says once more. This time it's low, and he drags the single word out with a growl. It is hands down the sexiest way anyone has ever said my name, and of course it came out of Luca's mouth.

I take a slow breath to control the way something so simple now makes my heart race and my mind imagine him saying my name in a completely different setting.

I bite my lip to keep from revealing the truth.

"I did not."

His gaze on me darkens as he steps closer. Slowly, he puts one hand on one side of my body and then does the same with the other, leaning in until we are so close our noses almost touch.

"I think you're lying to me."

"I …"

I could cry out in this situation, and it's not in the way you'd think. Well, unless you're thinking that I want him to close the gap and kiss me. That I want him to grab me, wrap my legs around his hips, and take my seat with me in his lap as he weaves his hands through my hair and I kiss him back.

I want that.

More than I've wanted anything from anyone before.

"Shay."

"Yeah?" It comes out in a breathy whisper.

My gaze flicks to his, but he's staring at my lips.

Oh god, does he want to kiss me back?

Suddenly, he pushes back and shakes his head.

"I need to get back to work."

I let out a breath and cup my forehead, and he walks away.

Holy shit.

"Right. Work."

He pauses then glances over his shoulder to stare at me again.

"Why did—" he starts, then stops. Again, he shakes his head.

"Ask me."

"What?"

I take a deep breath. I want to know what he was going to say, which is laughable because I normally don't, but it's clear something has shifted between us.

I'd be a fool not to acknowledge it now.

"Ask me what you were going to ask me."

His brow lifts and he thinks it over.

"Why did you lie about having a date in Wind Valley?"

"Because you make me nervous." The truth slips from my lips before I have time to overthink it.

Well, if things hadn't changed before, they sure as heck have now.

He nods, returning to stand in front of me.

His gaze sears into mine, and I know it's obvious that my breathing has picked up.

"The feeling is mutual," he admits and then backs up, hiking his thumb over his shoulder. "Want to lend me a hand with these arches?"

I nod, standing as if pulled by a string attached to Luca.

For the next hour, I help Luca put the arches up and try not to think too much about it when his hand touches mine or when he stands behind me, his chest to my back as he shows me exactly where I should place my hands to hold something while he gets the drill.

I try not to think about how I catch his gaze lingering on

me after I've done something he asked without arguing or when I find myself just standing there observing him.

No, I don't let myself think about any of it until we are walking out the door for the night.

"Thank you for getting the arches up tonight."

"I said I would."

"I know, it's just nice to work with someone who keeps their word."

"I always do."

I clear my throat.

"I'll be sure to tell Grace that fun fact about you."

He rubs the back of his neck.

"You don't need to do that."

"She'd probably like it. I mean, it's a nice—"

"No, I mean, you don't need to tell her anything. In fact, you can stop doing that."

I'm not sure I fully understand him. "Why?"

He shrugs. "Because you were right. We aren't a good match."

He heads for his truck with no more explanation.

I'd open my mouth to ask for more, but I'm not stupid.

I know why he doesn't want me to talk him up anymore, and I'm not mad about it.

I just don't know what it means to me to know this new fact.

Still, when he looks over his shoulder and winks at me, I roll my eyes.

It is Luca, after all.

I can't let him off that easily.

CHAPTER TWELVE

LUCA

Having a staff that works under you is great. It means shit gets done, but it doesn't mean that I get to slack off and do whatever I want all day long. Truth be told, right now, I wish I could just go back to sleep.

It's just after seven in the morning and my body hurts. I've been working double time. During the day, I stop by different sites to check in with my guys, and at night— well, Shay has my full attention. The last time I was working this hard was when I was trying to build my business.

And it hurts.

I think my age is showing. Thirties is not old, but damn, some days it sure feels like it.

I take another swig of my coffee and climb out of my truck, grabbing my tool bag.

Dutton Richford called me last night, leaving a voicemail to let me know that one of the weddings they had got a little rowdy and someone punched a hole through the wall.

I could tell he was fuming from how slow he spoke.

The Richfords set standards for Lovers Lodge, and when a guest does not meet those, he's never happy.

I get it.

If someone were on my property, I'd expect them to treat it with respect too.

The automatic doors open and I stride in, spotting Grace instantly.

I hold my cup up in greeting and make my way to her.

"Morning, Grace. Is your brother around?"

"Hi, Luca. It's early for you."

She crosses her arms and smiles.

"Yeah, but duty calls and I show up."

She nods slowly and then her smile grows.

"What?"

"Nothing." She shakes her head. "You seem different today."

"It's probably the lack of sleep. Your best friend keeps me up way too late and works me hard."

At that, Grace erupts into laughter.

"I … that came out wrong."

"It came out perfect, and I know what you meant." She winks, then points at the office behind us. "He's in there. Proceed with caution."

"You got it."

As I knock, waiting for Dutton to call me in, it occurs to me that I just held a conversation with Grace. There wasn't an ounce of nerves or hesitation or … a spark.

I felt nothing but the way I do as if I were speaking to Quinn or Sadie.

Huh.

I know I already told Shay she didn't need to hype me up anymore, but that just confirms it.

I'm not interested in Grace in any other way than as friends.

I'm not even fully sure why I asked her out at this point. My brothers were dating and they were happy, and I wanted it too, I guess.

You can't force a connection with someone.

She was right to turn me down.

"Come in!"

I open the door slowly. Dutton is sitting behind a large mahogany desk, pinching the spot between his eyes.

"I'd ask if things are good, but the vibe in this room is painful, so I'm not going to ask that."

"You're friends with Brooke, right?"

I make a yikes face and volley my head. "I mean, I know her fairly well, and she's good friends with Sadie and now Quinn, so sure, I guess."

"Why is she the way that she is?"

I wait for him to elaborate, but it's clear he's not going to.

"Um, what exactly did she do?"

"A bride this fall wants to rent B's Bakery for an entire day, and Brooke told me no."

"Oh."

I know I should have a better response, but it is her bakery. She makes the call.

"She's the only person who tells me no as if it's the simplest thing in the world. And not to mention, all I wanted the other night was one of her caramel brownies, and she wouldn't even let me through the door. I have no idea how I pissed her off, but she's not getting over it, and I … shit, this is not why you're here. Follow me."

He stands quickly and leads me to one of the reception halls. The hole in the wall—well, all three—are hard to miss.

"Why three?"

I wait for him to answer, studying him. He now has his hands on his hips, his glare set on the wall in question.

"Someone said they wanted to see who could make a bigger hole."

I pinch my lips together so that I don't laugh.

Instead, I cast my vote.

"It's the middle one."

"I agree. Now please fix it. We have another wedding tonight."

"You got it." I set my things down to get to work.

Dutton moves to leave, but then stops.

"I think we should have another boys' night sooner than planned."

I can't help but grin. I knew they had fun.

"I'll send a text."

"Good. Thank you."

I nod then do my thing fixing the wall.

People come and go, decorating for the couple of the evening. I let someone know that the paint still needs to dry, then I head back to the office to finish a few other things for the day before I meet Shay.

Shay.

Fuck.

Last night was … interesting.

In a roundabout way, we both admitted to having some type of feeling for the other. Yet, neither of us made a move to do anything about it.

Impressive restraint on my part, considering I've been wrestling with these feelings for a couple of days now.

It's like one moment my brain snapped, and now that I know I like her, I crave her. Seeing her, hearing her, being near her. Which is insane. It's not like I know what she tastes like or what she feels like under my fingertips.

I wish I did though.

As I drive down Main Street, I spot Shay walking out of one of the boutique shops. She's got a plant tucked under one arm and a reusable bag that looks full in the other. Mrs. Whittaker is walking toward her, and Shay stops to talk as I slow to the one and only traffic light this street has.

My eyes never leave her as I wait to go.

But then the light turns green, and the moment my truck inches forward, Shay looks in my direction. She smiles for the briefest of moments and bites her lower lip as she nods at me.

Fuck.

If I thought last night was a test of my restraint, tonight is going to be on a whole new level.

I'M NERVOUS.

I gaze out the front window of my truck at The Marina.

I can't remember the last time I was this nervous around a woman. Hell, even with Grace, I wasn't nervous. I just didn't know what to say.

Right now, I know a hundred things I could say. I

just don't know how I want to say them or how I can say them without sounding like I'm some lovestruck fool. Because let's be real here. Admitting to yourself that you have feelings for someone is one thing, but admitting to someone that you have feelings for them is really putting yourself out there. It's risky. Now the ball is in her court.

What's she going to do about it?

Does she even want to do anything about it?

What are my rules now?

I pick up my phone and stare at it, debating whether I should call Hudson.

He'd have advice for me. But really, Miles is the one I go to about this stuff.

I tap the contacts button and find his name, but then I click out and toss my phone to the passenger seat.

I don't need advice right now. I need to go inside and get to work, let her lead the room.

I nod, as if I need the gesture to convince myself that's what I should do.

Then I get out before I can second-guess myself anymore for the night.

When I reach the door, it swings open.

Shay is standing on the other side, and she gasps, stepping back when she sees me.

"Oh, hi."

"Hi."

"I thought maybe you weren't coming." She looks at her watch. "You're usually inside by now."

She looks at my lips, then at the floor before her gaze finds mine again.

It doesn't take me long to decide how I want to go about this.

I'm an open guy. I speak my mind. Sometimes it works out, and sometimes it doesn't. But with Shay, I don't want to be anyone but me. That's who she's been working with these last few weeks. That's who she deserves right now.

So I let out a breath and say, "I was working up the nerve to come inside."

Her gaze snaps to mine, and just like she did earlier today, she tugs that plump pink bottom lip into her mouth and bites it.

I think I growl, but I can't be sure. This urge is new for me.

"I was afraid you weren't coming," she admits. "And I was going to come find you."

My lips tug up, but I control it as her head tilts and she glares.

"Good to know," I say.

She nods then rolls her eyes. "Let's get to work."

It's probably best.

This whole calm conversation where we don't fight but we insinuate our attraction is getting me worked up.

I follow her into the main room, already loving the way we have reframed some of the walls in here. You can see the changes already, and even though it's not done, I feel pride and a weird amount of cockiness knowing that Shay won't ever be able to walk into the place without thinking of me again.

"I bought paint today so I could start on the hallways while you're finishing the walls in the dining room."

"I can help you paint if you want," I say, spotting her paint brushes and trays in a corner. "I also have sprayers I could bring tomorrow to make it go faster. If we want this room done within the week, I think using our time effectively is smart."

She stops walking and I bump into her.

"You really do want this place to be like it was when we were kids, don't you?"

"I said I did, didn't I?"

"Well, yeah, but you talk a lot." She smirks.

Oh, we've moved from banter to teasing, huh?

"Everything that comes out of these lips is true, Shay. Haven't you figured that out by now?"

"I am, yeah."

Then she winks at me and keeps walking.

My heart jumps, as if I need to be alerted that she's openly flirting with me.

I can't help but grin as I watch her walk away from me.

"What if we went to look at the cabins tonight? I know there are ten of them, and with everything else we have going on, it will be impossible to finish them by the end of summer, but maybe we could knock out a few."

"I could get more done if you let me work during the day."

Silence.

I want to say more or ask about why this is still an issue, but I don't.

It might be stupid, but it's what she wants, so I'm just going to keep going with it.

"Yeah, let's go look at them," I say instead.

"Really?" She looks over her shoulder, and her face lights up. "Now?"

I nod.

Her pace picks up and her hips sway faster.

Hell, if I'd known this was the view I'd be getting, I'd have suggested the cabins sooner.

We walk out the back door of The Marina and follow the stone pathway to where the cabins sit just off to the right. As Shay said, there are ten of them. They vary in size from one bedroom to two—a few offer extra beds for families. Some even have living rooms, and the one farthest away has a cozier vibe for couples who come for a weekend getaway.

We stop at the first one.

It's a one bedroom, so it's easy to write down the changes Shay wants to see. We make our way down the row quickly, spending a little longer in each cabin as they get larger.

Finally, we start to make the trek to the last cabin.

It's more secluded than the others for obvious reasons. I could easily sneak into this one during the day to work and no one would see me.

"I should start here," I suggest the moment the thought comes to mind.

"Why?"

"I could sneak in during the day with this one."

Shay unlocks the door, and as both step in, I can see instantly that it needs the same changes the others do, but the floor looks like it needs replacing, too.

I rub the back of my neck as I think of how to phrase my next question.

"How did these get so run-down?"

Shay runs her hand over the dresser and then looks at me through the mirror.

"I think my parents were slowly letting their dream go

while I was away at college. Then they let Leo take over." She lets out a sad laugh. "He obviously didn't care for this place. Add in the weather Wyoming gets throughout the year and the fact that the last time this cabin was rented was more than four years ago, time just … changed it."

I nod, the sadness in her tone hitting me right in the chest.

I'd been here the entire time she was away and never noticed how far the place was going in the wrong direction. Maybe if I'd tried to mend things with Leo, I could have reached out to Shay sooner.

I know this decay isn't my fault in any way, but at one time this place was like a home to me and a small part of me feels like I failed it.

"Well," I say and swing my gaze from the chipped door frames back to hers in the mirror. "I think the right person is in charge now and the comeback is going to be epic."

Her lips twist as she fights a smile.

"Thank you."

Even at this time of night, it's beginning to get hot inside the cabins, so I back up and point over my shoulder with my thumb. "Do you want the same changes here as the others or more?"

"More." Her eyes widen. "I want it to be more romantic. I want a door put in on this wall that leads to a private patio, too."

I look at the big wall. There isn't even a window in it, so her idea will work well and add more character to the room.

"I can do that."

"Great."

She rattles off a few other ideas that I agree to because she's smart and has a vision I'm determined to bring to life.

"Anything else?" I ask.

"I don't think so. Let me look at the bedroom real quick."

I follow her down the small hallway, the same way I have with all the other cabins.

Once she steps inside the room, she asks, "Do you think this bed is big enough?"

I glance at the mattress. It's a pretty basic queen with a comforter covered with pastel hearts, but it's big enough for two adults. Like Shay and I, for example, and suddenly the fact that we are standing alone in a room with a bed that has plenty of room to do all the things I could ever want to do to her is all my mind can focus on.

Shay on her back, her hands in my hair as I kiss every inch of her body.

Me on my back as Shay straddles my hips and …

"Luca?"

"What?"

"Is it big enough?"

"For what?" I ask quickly, to stay on task and not let my mind start dreaming again.

"For … sleeping."

I chuckle.

"Oh, it's big enough for sleeping," I wink. "And then some."

I guess those ideas aren't gone completely yet.

"Luca!"

"What you asked."

"Not everything has to have a sexual innuendo tied to it."

"Maybe not, but it's more fun that way."

She laughs, and I can't help but smile at her.

I like this side of Shay.

The side that likes me.

The side that doesn't want to fight with me.

I want to keep this side of her.

"I won't tell anyone, Shay."

"Tell anyone what?"

"That you want to be friends with me."

A slow smile touches her perfect pink lips. She shifts her gaze to me, the cutest wrinkle taking place between her eyes. As soon as they lock onto mine, my heart beats harder. Whatever she's about to say, she's going to try to get a rise out of me, and I know without a doubt it's going to work.

"Is that what you want, Luca? To be *friends* with me?"

Her left brow arches at the word *friends* while her focus drifts down to my mouth.

Kiss her, you dumbass.

Do it.

Stop playing this game with her.

"No. It's not."

Her eyes go wide.

She wasn't expecting me to say that. To be so blunt.

So before she can let her imagination run away with what I mean, I decide to show her instead.

I slide a hand around her back and yank her toward me, soaking in the way her mouth parts on a gasp.

"I could never just be friends with a woman like you, Shay."

My lips are on hers before she has a chance to reply.

They're just as soft as I knew they would be, but the moan that comes with it, vibrating against my tongue, urges me to act as if I'm starving for her touch. I back her up until she hits the dresser, then I slip my tongue past her lips. She meets mine with her own. Ohhhhh. Damn, she tastes like sugar. Her hands skim up the front of my shirt, scorching my body with her fingertips, and I press into her, letting her feel how hard she's made me from just one touch.

She breaks the kiss to take a deep breath, but she doesn't let go of me, so I kiss her neck, memorizing her every feature as I reach her collarbone.

"Luca," she whimpers, and I lose it.

In a frenzy, I grip her hips and set her on the dresser. My hands instinctively cup her knees and spread her legs, then I stand between them and tug her to me.

I grind into her and take her lips with mine once more.

With both hands now on her ass, I spread my fingers wide, lifting her slightly to rub her against me.

"Fuck," I say.

"I know."

For a split second, I think she's going to agree with me only to push me away and say we can't do this, but she doesn't. Instead, she holds my face in her hands and kisses me harder.

I'm not going to fuck her the first time I kiss her, but fuck all if my dick isn't begging me to move this along faster right now.

But then someone honks their horn, and we both split away from each other.

The room suddenly feels small as our chests heave and we catch our breaths.

I meet her eyes, only to notice her red and swollen lips.

Those are my lips.

Then she drops her gaze and stares at my cock, which is fully erect right now thanks to her.

She steps back and says the words I dreaded to hear a moment ago.

"That can never happen again."

And then she dashes out of the room and out of the cabin.

Well, that's fucking great.

Not.

CHAPTER THIRTEEN

SHAY

The Marina is my focus.

The Marina is my focus.

The Marina is my focus.

This is the phrase I've repeated all day long. And it was a lot, too, because today was slow and I hated every minute of it. It only reminded me that this is all the more reason why whatever happened with Luca last night can't happen again.

Even if every single part of my body is crying for it.

Shit.

I've never felt like this over someone.

No one has ever kissed me like that before.

It's all so … so … perfect.

"Shay, hey," a voice pulls me from my thoughts, and I spot Ruby Asher walking toward me, holding her son, Max's, hand. They are both in swimwear and look ready for a day in the sun.

"Ruby!" I beam and then move to the other side of the counter to hug her. I ruffle Max's hair, and he swats me away.

I chuckle when he smiles up at me.

"I didn't know you were back in town," I say.

"We actually moved back yesterday. Only my dad knows right now."

"Oh" is all I say. I start to say more, but her eyes flash to her son—a hint not to ask more questions. She'd been visiting a lot this summer, but moving back after all these years is huge.

Fun fact about me and Ruby…while I was away at college, Ruby and Max's father were living in the same town as me because she attended the same college. We saw each other weekly, but never told anyone because of our family situation. It was nice to hang out where we didn't have to worry about the town gossip.

That said, I'm still beyond thrilled that she's back. I did miss her.

"Well, it sounds like you two could use a moving break to have some fun today."

"That's the plan." Ruby grins. "Any chance you have a paddleboard for rent today?"

"I do!"

She's being modest. This place is like a ghost town today.

I quickly ring her up. Then I signal to Carl to take over for me as I walk her outside.

Max runs ahead of us.

"Is everything okay?" I ask.

She nods. "Colter and I just finally agreed we are better off as friends. The moment I suggested moving back to raise Max here, he didn't even argue."

"Oh. Are you okay with that?"

"Of course. I think we are on good terms, but I do feel like

I should be annoyed that he didn't fight harder to keep Max close to him. It's like, I would have been furious if he objected, because this is where Max and I belong, but at the same time, why didn't he argue to keep his son closer?"

I can't even begin to understand how she feels.

"That would be hard," I say, " but I think you both being here is the best."

"Me too. And his dad already has plans to visit, so I think it'll be great."

"Good."

"And I missed you and everyone here, and everything already feels right, so I don't know why I'm complaining."

"Stop, don't ever feel guilty for worrying."

She hugs me. "This is what I missed. Okay, remind me how to do this."

I run her through some basic instructions then wave as she and Max get going. His laughter is all I hear as I head back to The Marina.

But then I see a familiar truck drive by toward the cabins, and I pick up my steps.

"He wouldn't," I whisper to no one.

I practically sprint past all the cabins until I get to the last one.

Sure enough, there is Luca's truck backed between two trees. Yeah, okay, you'd have to be standing right where I am to see it, but that's not the point.

I march up to the door and storm in, slamming it shut.

"Shit." Luca spins around, his hand flying to his chest. "You scared me."

"I told you not to come here during the day."

He sighs. "I'm just trying to get some things done."

"Well, do it later."

"I'll be like fifteen minutes."

"No."

"Damnit, Shay, just let me do this real quick."

"Why?"

"Because I fucking want to make you happy. Jesus. And having these cabins finished will do that, so just let me do my job."

I pull back as if he slapped me.

Oh.

"Okay" is all I can think to say.

"Okay."

Then I rush out so I don't do something stupid like kiss him again, because after a comment like that, how could I not want to jump into his arms?

This is bad. So, so bad.

Kissing Luca Asher is a recipe for disaster, and I can't afford to do anything that could jeopardize finishing this place.

I want to make you happy.

Ugh.

Swoon.

Shit.

Luca!

TRUE TO HIS WORD, Luca finished whatever he needed in the cabin and left for the day. Now, the sun has gone down, leaving only its scorching heat as any sign that it was here today.

I glance out the back windows of The Marina, pulling my hair into a messy bun to keep it from sticking to my neck as I watch Luca's truck pull into the parking lot.

He gets out, takes a deep breath, then grabs a bag and makes his way toward the cabins again.

Last I knew, we were still working inside the main dining room tonight.

It's possible he's trying to avoid me.

I wouldn't fault him for that. Our last two interactions have been hotter than this day, but still, I want to stick to a schedule. The dining room is more important to me than the cabins right now.

I head for the door, only for it to swing open, Luca stepping through like a man on a mission.

He freezes when he sees me, and I do the same.

"I was going to start in the cabin because I've thought of nothing but you all day and I wanted a little space to figure it out. But I know this room is important, so here I am."

My lips twitch.

Has he always been this cute?

It's scary how attuned he is to my brain.

Is that a sign?

A sign for what, Shay?

"That's a good plan," I say, because, oh my gosh, why do I not know how to act around him right now?

I spin for the dining room, feeling his eyes on me as he follows, sending goose bumps all over my skin.

We both get to work without another word.

Luca turns on some music, and I'm thankful for it. The silence in the room was putting me on edge, which is crazy considering the words we've left unspoken have created tension thick enough to soundproof these walls.

Oh my god.

What am I saying?

My brain has officially tripped a wire.

"Beautiful Things" by Benson Boone comes on, and of course, *of course*, Luca starts to sing along to it. Now, I'm not saying that he has the voice of an angel by any means, but it's deep and smooth and soothing.

One kiss and I'm just completely gone for him.

This is nuts.

"I'm going out to the truck to grab the paint sprayer so you can start in the hallway if you want."

"Great. Thanks," I say quickly and then just stand there.

I'm making this more weird between us.

Can he sense that I just want to jump him?

Oh.

My.

God.

Why is my brain like this right now?

As soon as he returns, he helps me get the sprayer all set up.

"Just go slow. Like this." He shows me just how slow I need to go and then hands me the sprayer. I start, but it isn't what I'm expecting, and I mess up right away, leaving a splotch on the wall.

"Shoot," I say, and he chuckles.

"Here, I'll show you again."

He steps up behind me and gently places his hands on mine.

With his front flush to my back, I close my eyes. I know this isn't supposed to be romantic, but the moment his arms wrap around me, my body instantly relaxes and I let out a breath.

"Shay." His breath wisps across the skin of my neck, causing my nipples to alert me to his presence. As if I didn't know where he was already.

"Pay attention."

"I am."

"From the way your ass is pushing into my cock right now, I'd be confident to argue that."

I moan. His sultry voice is hypnotizing.

The moment his lips touch my neck, I snap my eyes open and duck out of his arms.

"I …"

The words don't come to me, but after a few seconds, Luca nods as if he gets it.

"It's stupid hot in here. I need to cool down."

He walks away from me and out to the deck that's blocked off from guests so that they don't mess up his markings for new boards. Next week is our goal to finish that project, but that's not the point right now. Right now, the point is that I've never seen Luca this flustered.

And the most shocking part of it? He's quiet.

I watch him pace the deck.

He pauses with his back to me as he runs his hand through his hair.

It was one kiss.

How can we both be so worked up about it?

I mean, sure, it was soft and sexy at the same time. It was captivating and took my breath away. It was mind-blowing and addicting.

And, as Luca clearly wants, I want it to happen again.

I do.

But it can't.

Things are complicated enough with him working here and me keeping that a secret. If we start anything more, it would just be a fire.

And I do not doubt that everything would go up in flames. I can't afford for The Marina to suffer once more because of a choice I made.

I turn my gaze away from the windows and fail to find something in the room to focus on.

I glance back to where Luca is standing, He's watching me.

That look—ohhhh, that look.

I've never had someone look at me like that before.

Like he can't look away even if he tried.

Like he's never wanted anything more than what's standing in front of him.

And for Luca, that something is me.

I give my head a small shake and shrug.

This only fuels his frustration even more.

He quickly moves to the steps that lead to the beach.

It's after ten, so the beach is closed right now, but that doesn't stop him.

"Where are you going?" I yell from the deck.

"To cool off."

"Where?"

He pauses, turns, and then reaches behind him to pull his shirt off.

"In the water, Shay. I think we both need it. I'd ask you to join me, but we both know the answer."

He can't be serious. Swimming, now? And what does that mean, we know the answer. One kiss doesn't mean he knows me. Yet … he sort of does.

I have control, but I am a woman with needs, and that right there would be testing it to its ma—oh my gracious goodness golly, there go his pants.

He's in his underwear.

Boxer briefs.

I should have known.

Look how they hug his hips. How they hug his thick thighs and how—

"Are you going to stand there and watch me swim or prove me wrong and start stripping?"

I roll my eyes and cross my arms.

"It's not safe to swim this late, Luca. You know this."

"All the more reason not to let me swim alone."

"I'm not getting in."

"Fine. If I start to drown or whatever, you better hustle from your perch on that deck."

He's not going to drown.

Said way too many people before something went bad.

I jog down the steps.

"I'm only coming down here so that I can save you when you need it."

He grins, and I swear to god, he may as well have touched me between my legs.

Shit.

No. This is not good.

"You okay?" Luca asks as he walks backward and slowly into the water.

"Fine."

"You're flushed."

"It's too dark for you to see that."

He shrugs but chuckles when I don't tell him he's wrong.

"You could get in here and cool down with me, then we get back to work."

"Luca."

"Okay. Okay. You're right. I'm done."

He dips lower into the water but never takes his eyes off me.

"Stop watching me."

He grins and turns. Then he dunks under the water.

I glance at The Marina and then back at the water.

We *are* alone.

So, I mean, no one would know except us.

And, I've never … been in my underwear in public. I don't have a bucket list or anything, but the idea of it does give me a rush I didn't expect.

Luca keeps treading water and ignoring me like I asked, and it annoys me even more.

He just keeps listening to me, and it's starting to piss me off.

It's not okay for him to be this attentive to me.

To me.

Me!

This is not what we do, and yes, I know things are changing, but when the summer is over and it's time for my family to return, I need us to be the old Shay and Luca. Not … whatever this is.

When the summer is over.

It's not over yet.

And getting whatever this is out of my system could be a

good idea. He's probably all talk anyway and it wouldn't even be that great.

I stomp my foot as if someone said something to upset me, and technically they did, only it was me.

Am I really considering this?

The urge to do something crazy and just let my mind relax for once is consuming.

Before I can think twice, I pull my shirt over my head and slip off my shorts.

Then I run toward the water before Luca can turn around and see me. I would have made it if not for my squeal the entire way.

He spins quickly, the grin on his face dropping quickly when he spots me.

I wade in and then tread toward him. Once I'm right in front of him, I'm taken back at how dark his eyes have turned under the moonlight. At how they are locked right on mine with a hunger I've never seen in them before.

Now my heart is racing, and my body is heating up even though I'm in the cool water.

Why won't he look away?

"Stop looking at me like that."

"Like what?" He asks, his voice raspy.

My heart pounds.

"Like … bad decisions are about to be made."

"By whom? Me?"

"By both of us."

My admission doesn't help the situation, and frankly, at this point, who am I trying to fool?

Luca treads closer but stops, as if he's trying to talk himself out of it.

"Isn't that why you got in the water?"

Yes.

I should tell him to move back.

But I can't.

I swim closer.

He reaches a hand out and slides it around my hips under the water, pulling me to his body. My fingers lock around his neck as soon as my lips crash against his.

The hand that tugged me close wraps around my lower back, and his other hand cups the side of my face. I lock my legs around him to hold on and let the small waves of the lake create the remainder of the movement for us.

I feel him harden instantly against the thin fabric of my panties, and I let out a strangled noise.

Fuck.

He breaks the kiss to press his lips to my cheek, chin, and neck, then adjusts his hands so that one is holding onto my hips. Then he grinds me against him. Hard. He's huge.

"Oh, god," I breathe.

I withdraw my joke about him not being big enough. He might be too big.

And that makes my heart race even more.

"Do you like that?"

"Yes," I whisper. "So much."

Then I move my hips faster.

"Jesus, Shay," he says before he's kissing me again.

I love everything about it. The way his lips are soft but the pressure of the kiss is firm, as if he can't get enough of me.

This feeling of being wanted is addicting.

He moves my hips faster and faster.

"Luca," I whisper into his ear. "You …"

My words fade into the night air as tingles course through my body.

This man is about to make me come by rubbing me against this cock in the water. I've never come like this. My brain is scattered. I normally have to be focused and concentrate on my orgasm, but right now all I can think about is his hands and his lips and the way he's breathing in my air.

"Luca," I repeat again, because for the life of me I can't think of words.

"I know, baby, I hear you. I'm not letting you go until you get what you need."

I close my eyes, my nipples hardening at his promise, and just when I think it can't get any better, one of his hands slinks between my legs, moving my underwear to the side and sliding his fingers inside of me.

"Oh, god, yes, please. Don't stop. Please."

"Fuck, you're begging. I love it. Tell me what you need, baby. Ride my fingers. Take what you want from me, and if it's not enough when you're done, I'll slide my cock inside of you and fuck you until it is."

And just like that, my body convulses and my orgasm runs through my veins, screaming as if it never wants this feeling to end. My skin is on fire as he sets off every part of me.

I bite Luca's shoulder as wave after wave of release rushes through me, and after I feel confident that I can take over the control of my body once more, I slowly lift my head.

I don't have time to consider what the look in his eyes means before he's kissing me again.

He pulls back and rests his forehead against mine.

"Feel better?" he asks, and I laugh.

"Much."

"Good."

I let the water float me, and reach between us. I grip him in my hand, but he stops me.

"You don't have to do that."

"I want to," I say before he can go on. "I don't need the whole 'this is about you and only you and a lady should never have to blah. Blah' bullshit, Luca. Let me touch you."

He smirks, licks his lips, and nods.

"Whatever you want, baby. It's yours."

God, I didn't know how much I'd love it when he says things like that to me.

I stroke him, keeping our gazes locked.

I start slowly, letting my thumb run over the tip, and I can't help but smile the moment his eyes roll back.

"Do you like that?" I repeat his words back to him.

"Fuck, Shay, don't talk dirty to me."

"Why? You don't want to hear the way I love how you feel in my hand?"

He groans.

"How you made me come harder than anyone before you."

Another groan.

"How I want to trace every inch of you with my fingers. Maybe even my tongue."

"I'm going to come."

"That's the plan. Do it. Come in my hand."

He grabs my face and kisses me. As he comes, he pulls my bottom lip between his teeth and growls.

I keep stroking him until he pulls away.

"Damn it."

"What?" I let out a little laugh.

Under the moonlight, his gaze finds mine.

"You know I won't be able to keep my hands off you now, right?"

I grin. Yes, tonight changed everything between us.

"I know."

And I don't want him to.

Not now or at the end of the summer.

Which is a problem.

A very big problem.

CHAPTER FOURTEEN

LUCA

Pounding on a door before the sun has fully risen should be illegal.

I march to my front door, my steps heavy. Yeah, I'm tired, but it was worth it.

Last night was one of the latest nights I've spent working with Shay.

We didn't talk about the lake, but we did steal touches once we made it back inside, dried off, and got to work. I even kissed her goodnight. I don't know what it means yet, but I knew the moment she hit the water that if she was going to give me a chance, I wouldn't ruin it by not getting work done at The Marina.

So yeah, I stayed later than usual, and aside from paint, new furniture, and finishing touches, the dining room is ready.

I'm not sure which made her smile more, the way I made her come in the water or seeing her dream come to life.

Probably a mix of both.

The pounding resumes, followed by "Luca! Open the door!"

Oh, it's my brother. Perfect. Our schedules haven't let us see each other much lately, and I—

"Luca, open the goddamn door!"

Oh, someone's touchy.

In nothing but my gym shorts, I swing the door open to see a panicked Miles.

"Jesus, some of us do sleep in the morning. We can't all be workaholics like you."

Which is funny because I sort of am as of lately.

"We need to talk." He marches right past me to my kitchen.

"O-kay, what's wrong with you?" I ask, following him.

"Oh, what's wrong with me? So, so many things." He drops to sit in one of my kitchen table chairs, cradling his face. "Where do I start?"

"There's a whole story? Hell yes." I clap and start to make some coffee. It's not Brooke's, but it will have to do for now.

"So, you know my thing with Cherry, right?" he starts.

The number one reason we avoid hooking up with tourists. Of course I know her.

"Yep."

"You know I wanted to avoid her."

Because Miles forgot about our number one rule last summer.

"Yep."

"Well, turns out Quinn wanted to avoid some guy, too."

"Who?"

"Doesn't matter."

"It matters to me."

I need details. Does he not know me?

"Still doesn't matter. Anyway, she told her friends, who I don't think she should call that, that she was dating me."

"What? She just made it up when she saw them?" I chuckle.

He shakes his head.

"No, she told them last summer."

He lost me already. Last summer? That's odd.

"You've been dating since last summer?"

"No. Pay attention."

I hold my hands up in surrender. It's early, and this is a lot to take on with my own Shay thing going on.

"I'm trying."

"She told her … people that she was dating me so that they'd stop trying to set her up with this guy. Fast forward to this summer and those people show up here to get married at the lodge, so Quinn came to me with a plan that both validates her story and helps me keep Cherry away."

"And that was …"

"To fake date. We are fake dating."

"I fucking knew it!" I stand so fast that my chair flips onto its back. "There was no way she fell for your grumpy ass that fast. Not to mention, you're always a dick to her."

All right, so I didn't know they were fake dating, but I knew something was up with them.

"Anyway," he goes on, "the fake dating thing has been working out, and Quinn even devised a plan to set Cherry up with the guy she's avoiding."

He's setting Cherry up with who?

"Whoa, whoa, so you—"

"But the reason I'm here is because we kissed last night."

My jaw drops.

"And there may have been more than kissing."

My eyes go wide.

"We may have taken our clothes off."

I slap my forehead.

"And I want to do it again."

My hands cover my ears.

Holy shit. Holy. Shit. Miles and I are basically having the same problem over the same summer, minus the whole fake dating part of it.

Fuck.

Look at us, out here kissing these women and having not a clue how to handle it.

I open my mouth and then close it, pacing the kitchen.

Is this a twin thing? We both changed the course of our relationship with the enemy on the same night.

This would be a good time to tell him about me and Shay, except ... she still doesn't want people to know that I'm coming to The Marina to help her. It's a given that she'd not want people to know anything more.

Shit. That sucks.

"So, are you still fake dating?" I ask, keeping the conversation on him.

"Yep."

"But not fake fooling around?"

"Is that a thing?"

"I don't know, Miles. You tell me. I didn't think fake dating was a real thing until just now. That's movie shit. Not real life."

"That's what I told her."

"And yet here you are." I put my hands on my hips and shake my head. We really are quite the set of twins here. "Wow. And we thought I was the one to make rash choices."

"I came here for help, not for you to point out my current flaws."

I grin. "This isn't a flaw. In fact, I think it's great."

The same way I think my thing with Shay is. We just clearly have to help our ladies to see that.

"What? How? I just screwed everything up between us."

I lean against the counter and nod toward the coffee pot. "How so?"

Miles makes himself a cup of coffee and says, "Because we were supposed to fake date and then break up, it was an easy plan. Fooling around and oral sex was not part of the plan."

"Whoa, spare me the details."

"I just think you need to know details to see the full depth of this fuckup."

"You didn't fuck up, but," I say and then stop, the biggest smile forming on my face. "I do love the dramatics right now. Is this how you feel when I talk to you?"

It's been a while since Miles came to me with this much information, and I like it.

"Luca, I need you to be serious."

"I am. I don't think you fucked up, Miles. You've had a crush on her since the first day you saw her. I'd say this whole thing is overdue. You just had to fake date to get there."

He groans. "I don't think you get it."

"No, I don't think you do. An opportunity was given to you, and you need to open your eyes to figure out what it is and take it before it's gone. Now you have two choices: see where this thing goes with Quinn or call the entire thing off. I think we both know which path you're going to take."

He nods, soaking in my words.

For the first time in I don't know how long, I decide to take my own advice.

Somehow Shay and I were meant to work on The Marina together. Whether it was to mend a friendship or to be whatever we are becoming.

Either way, I know I need to be patient and find out.

For Shay, the risk is worth it.

———

MY STOMACH IS a bundle of nerves as I make my way into The Marina.

My instinct tells me to just walk in and kiss her because, hell, I've been thinking about her all day. In fact, she's done nothing but consume my every waking thought for the past few days.

I don't mind it one bit.

I'm eager to see her smiling face right now, and I'm going to make sure she knows it.

With the dining room and main hallway basically finished, I plan to get started on the area she wants done in the store. Hopefully, the cabins are next week, but the more I think about it, I should suggest extending the deck to a full wrap-around to the parking lot main door.

I pause outside the back door and take a breath.

But as soon as I step in, one thing is clear.

Shay isn't here.

If it weren't for the fact that I'm early, I'd say she was avoiding me after last night.

But fuck, last night was phenomenal.

I had no idea I could feel like that with someone.

Of course it's Shay.

I have no idea if this means we're starting something or if it'll just be for fun or if she's going to tell me again that she thinks it was a mistake and she never wants it to happen again.

I groan.

I don't want her to tell me that last part.

Being near Shay is different from the way we started and it isn't just because of the way she argued with me on everything. It was how she just made my life more exciting.

I don't want that to go away, but I also don't know how we are going to navigate this.

I start moving things around in the shop to prepare for what needs to be moved to the cabins so I'm not hauling things back and forth constantly. Our new relationship won't change anything about my commitment. About twenty minutes in, I hear a noise in the parking lot.

Moving to check it out, I spot Shay, Sadie, and Brooke.

All three women are giggling as they share hugs. I stand in the doorway, leaning on the frame.

Now, I knew they were all friends, but they don't normally blast it on account of the fact that Shay's family doesn't care for me or mine now and Sadie is dating my brother, but to see her with my future sister-in-law makes me like her even more.

They look so comfortable around each other. She'd fit in with my family perfectly.

Which is crazy to think about.

We've kissed twice, plus a little more, and haven't even had sex. Yet, here I am thinking of how, despite that, I know I need her in my life.

Suddenly, the laughter stops and all three women are staring at me.

"Ladies." I walk toward them.

Brooke pushes Shay gently from behind.

Sadie waves from behind Shay, who has completely stolen my attention.

She's wearing a pair of cutoff jean shorts like usual and a T-shirt that hangs off her shoulder. Today's heat is still high, so her messy bun falls around her face, a strand of hair here and there sticking to her cheek.

I grin as she blushes, her eyes never leaving mine.

"Hi," she says.

"Hi."

I can't help it. I chuckle.

It's not even weird. Instead, it's like this greeting is just a tease for the tension that will build up tonight.

I hope we get work done, but I hope we don't. The look she's giving me makes me want to grab her and kiss her, and I don't care who's watching.

She rolls her eyes, the same as she's always done, but this time there is a pink tint on her cheeks as she passes me.

I glance over my shoulder to make sure she gets inside safely and then I look back at Sadie. Brooke's already back in the car.

"Thank you for driving her."

"Of course. We got carried away, and I didn't want her walking."

"I appreciate that."

I expect Sadie to get into her car as well, but instead she stands there, smiling at me.

"What?"

"I don't know."

"Okay." I chuckle and then take a step backward. "I better get to work."

She waves, but as soon as I turn, she calls out my name.

"Yeah?"

"I don't know what is going on with you two, but I like it."

I just smile. Normally, I'd have something, anything to say. I'd possibly go off on a tangent of how I have no idea what's happening and I need to know because that's how my brain works, but as much as I adore Sadie, she's not the woman I should be having that conversation with.

"I like it, too. Good night, Sadie."

I make my way inside to find Shay just standing in the middle of the small store.

"You decided to start in this room tonight?"

I scratch the back of my neck as she looks around the room.

"Yeah, I just figured that, even though some of the other rooms are waiting on a few things before you finish painting and whatnot, this room needed attention. I want to get it done the right way."

Shay turns slightly, looking over her shoulder. "Don't do that."

The words sound like scolding, but I barely hear them slip from her lips.

"Do what?"

"Understand me."

I grin, but then she glares, and I correct my expression quickly.

"Well, I just want your vision to come true."

She stomps her foot. "Don't do that either."

"What?" I chuckle.

"Be cute and stuff."

"Well, then stop making me like you," I argue back. I cross my arms and wait for her to say something else that's snappy and witty and makes me want her more than I already do. If that's even possible.

"Do you always just say whatever comes to mind?"

I nod. "I don't see the point in beating around the bush or whatever you want to call it, and I hate reading between the lines."

I step toward her.

"Must be refreshing."

"It is. You should try it."

I take another step, and this time she mirrors me.

"And say what?"

"Whatever is on your mind."

We are toe to toe now. Her head tilts back to look up at me.

"Are you sure you want that?"

Considering we were both half naked and wet in the water last night, yeah, I do. Still, I swallow, worried she might tell me that this is all wrong, but by the way her eyes shine, I don't think that's the case here.

"I've never been more sure."

She waits a beat and then whispers, "I want you to

kiss me."

I do it in an instant, cupping her face in my hands as I press my lips to hers.

She stands on the tips of her toes, her hands clenching my shirt at the sides as she slips her tongue into my mouth.

She tastes just as good as I remember.

"What are we doing?" she asks, breaking the kiss and resting her forehead on mine. "If your whole thing is to be completely honest, I need to know."

I pull back to look her in the eyes.

They are filled with as much worry as I've felt in the last twenty-four hours.

"I don't know yet, but I know I don't want to stop kissing you. I know that it could get tricky. I know that despite that, I want to spend more time with you. I want to get to know you more. And I—"

"Oh my gosh, this is a lot."

I chuckle.

"And I know that, that right there, your sass—I fucking love it."

"You do?" She blushes.

"Oh yeah. It turns me on."

"Really?"

I nod.

"Our banter does that for me," she admits.

"Of course it does."

She rolls her eyes.

"It's because it's banter with me."

"Work first, play later," she says in a tone that makes me grow hard. She laughs and shoves me back.

At least she said we can play later.

"Anything you want, boss," I say with a wink and then get back to work. Shay heads for the paint sprayer I've already set up.

"I can feel you watching me."

"It's hard not to."

"Luca Asher, get to work now."

I groan.

I turn the music up. Maybe if I can't hear her moving around, I'll forget she's close by.

My dick twitches.

Probably not.

An hour later, I can't take it anymore.

She's just cleaning up her things when I walk in the room.

She looks up, our eyes lock, and I know in that moment that she knows I have no more control.

She meets me halfway, her arms swinging around my neck to kiss me back.

"I'm done working for tonight."

"Thank god," she breathes and tilts her head back so I can kiss her neck.

I have no idea how we are going to balance finishing The Marina and the cabins with this pull we have to each other, but I'm sure we will figure it out. It might take longer, but that's fine by me. It means more time with Shay.

"Hold on, hold on," Shay says and steps back.

She looks around the room as if someone is going to walk in at any moment.

"You're closed."

"I know," she says. "But maybe we should still go someplace else."

I raise a brow, waiting for her to go on.

"Walk me back to my place?"

I nod.

"Let's go."

She laughs, and I feel a little stupid for clearly sounding so eager, but screw it.

I like her and she likes me and we are both consenting adults.

She locks up, and as soon as we fall into step en route to her house, I lace her hand with mine.

I don't overthink it. I do it because it feels natural. I can't come up with any cons.

With a little tug, I pull her closer, and she loops one arm through mine for the block walk.

We walk in silence, which is crazy for us, but the tension between us is loud enough that talking would just be too much.

Once inside, Shay heads for the kitchen to grab a couple of bottles of water.

I'm standing in front of her photo wall when she returns to the living room.

I hadn't noticed all the pictures when I picked her up for that date night. I was too blown away by her being in the room with me, and I didn't know how to process it.

"I like this one," I say and raise a brow in question.

She looks at the photo of her and my sister and grins.

"I'm glad she's back."

Miles texted me a few hours ago to tell me Ruby moved back. He felt he needed to update me on how this means Dad is moving into the apartment Quinn was in and now Quinn is moving in with Miles.

I wish him luck, I'm not living with Shay, but just being near her sends my blood south.

"I am too. I do wonder about Max's dad, though."

"Ruby's a big girl. She's got this. Don't worry about her too much."

I pin Shay with a look.

"Did she tell you to say that, or are you speaking from experience?"

The latter.

She moves to the couch and sits.

"I don't think my family thinks I can turn The Marina around. No, I know they don't. My parents are still thinking about selling it."

"What?"

I join her on the couch, our knees touching. "When?"

"They haven't made an official decision, but this summer is pretty much the last chance it has. That *I* have."

" Why didn't you say something sooner?"

"I—" She cuts herself off and shakes her head with a firm smile. "It's not something I like to talk about."

She looks away quickly, tucking a loose hair behind her left ear. "How's the construction business going?"

How's the construction business going?

Is she for real right now?

I study her for a moment. She looks everywhere but at me.

She's not telling me something.

I want to ask her about it right now, but this is all new for us.

What's overstepping and what isn't?

"Business is good. Would have been better if you had hired me from the start."

She nods. "Agreed."

And then she looks at my lips while biting her lower one, and I can't do this small talk anymore.

I lean in to kiss her.

Shay doesn't just kiss me back—she crawls into my lap.

She straddles me, so I take full advantage and run my hands up her bare thighs until I reach her ass and give it a squeeze.

My dick grows immediately in my jeans, ready to pop the zipper like some teenager who has a girl in his lap for the first time.

Last night I had her against me in the water, and that was nice, but this right here, with nothing is between us, is killing me.

I love it.

She starts to grind her hips against me.

"Up," I command, and her body moves as if I'm pressing a button.

I flick the button of her shorts open and then tug.

"Take these off."

She climbs off me to do what I said, one hand holding onto my shoulder for balance.

Once they are disposed of, Shay is standing in front of me in nothing but a white lace thong and a cropped T-shirt. The same one that hangs off her shoulder, giving me a tease of how soft her skin is.

But it won't be a tease for much longer.

I lean forward, grip her behind her thighs, and plant her right back on my lap. This time, I put a hand between us so that I can touch her.

"Ohhh." She lets out on a shaky breath when I rub my fingers against her.

"Fuck, Shay, you're soaked."

"I know." She bites my shoulder again, and I decide that I like it when she does that. It's like she's so consumed by me and what I'm doing that she can't control herself.

I grab her face and press my lips to hers at the same time I slide a finger inside her.

Oh, hell. She's wet.

I did that.

I don't need to ask her if it was me. I know it was.

"Yeah, baby, this is how I want you from here on out."

"How?"

I slip another finger inside her.

"More, please."

"Wet, needy, and begging for more," I tell her and bite her earlobe.

It's not hard, but it's enough for her to let out a moan.

Leaning back, I whip her shirt over her head and discard her bra with the flick of a hand.

My mouth sucks one nipple between my lips while my fingers tug at the other.

"Jesus, Luca. I feel you everywhere."

"Oh, baby. If you think you can feel me now, wait until I'm inside you."

"Don't make me wait, please."

Her begging will be the death of me.

Because I want this night to last past one and done, I stand up and drop her back on the couch. I can see in her eyes that a protest is coming, so I beat her to the punch, spread her wide and lick her pussy in one long, slow stroke.

Her hands grip my hair and pull.

"Yes, Luca."

I keep going, and when her back bows off the couch, I know she's close.

So I hook my arms against her thighs and push my tongue as far inside her as it can go, and then join it with a finger.

I hook it up, and she combusts.

Her hips are uncontrollable as she rides my face.

"Luca, Luca, Luca!" she screams.

I can't help but grin when she stops moving. Her fingers still leisurely scratch at my head.

I look up to find her watching me with sedated eyes.

"I'm going to do that every single night," I tell her.

Her cheeks redden.

"Don't be shy on me now, Shay."

"I'm not. I'm just …" But she doesn't finish.

"You just what?" I ask.

"I'm happy right now." The smile she gives me is a first.

Fuck, and here I thought I was proud of making her scream my name.

Knowing I put that smile there makes my heart thud faster.

Then she yawns, and despite the major erection I have right now, she needs sleep. We both do.

I push off the couch and hand her her shirt.

"I'll, uh, see you tomorrow?" I ask and rub the back of my neck. I wasn't prepared for this part of the night.

"No," she says quickly.

Fuck. She's calling this already?

What can I say? How do I change her mind?

"You can stay the night," she adds and then yawns again.

"You need rest." I bend to kiss her forehead.

As much as I'd love to crawl into her bed with her and keep the both of us up all night long, I care more about her well-being.

"I know, but I want you to stay either way."

She gazes up at me, and if I didn't know it before, I know it now: whatever Shay asks of me, I'll do it.

CHAPTER FIFTEEN

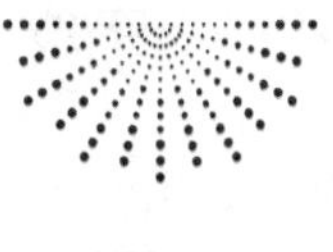

SHAY

After seeing Luca yesterday afternoon at The Marina, I'd gone to girls' night with the intention of telling them enough to get advice without sharing every detail. Especially since Ruby was there. Grace was gone, but it was like the girls knew this was going to happen all along, and we got carried away talking about Luca. By the time Sadie drove me to The Marina, I was determined not to let this get too far.

But then there he was, standing in the doorway of the place I love most in the world, looking as if he belonged there.

I knew at that moment that was a view I wanted to see day after day.

I let out a groan, because holy moly, complicated doesn't even begin to describe my life right now, and then I roll over, only to be stopped short when my sheets won't roll with me.

Slowly, I look over my shoulder to find a shirtless Luca sleeping next to me.

The entire night comes back to me. The way he kissed me

in the dining room. The way he walked me home. The way he laid me out on my couch, the way his hands felt as they brushed every inch of my body, me asking him to stay with the full intention of having sex with him—and me falling asleep within minutes of him wrapping his arm over my stomach.

It's been a long time since I fell asleep that quickly.

Slowly, I peel the covers away from my face and look at him.

His breathing is slow as he lays on his back, one hand resting over his head while the other is resting on his stomach.

Jesus. He's in shape. When does he even find the time?

Rock-solid abs stare back at me, and I love that there is a small bit of chest hair on his pecs. My eyes wander lower to the waistband of his boxers. I don't need to see them to know that's what he's wearing. The brand name around the waist is hint enough.

He looks so cute when he sleeps.

Innocent.

Ugh.

Crushing on Luca isn't good for me.

I slink out of bed and instantly notice my pajamas.

Or, well, Luca's shirt.

I tiptoe to the bathroom and close the door.

Looking in the mirror, my gaze drifts to the clothes, and without thinking twice, I pick at the shirt collar, pulling it over my nose to inhale.

It smells just like him.

What am I going to do? How do we go about this? Does he want to go about this?

I grab my toothbrush, brush my teeth, and then turn on the

shower. When the water is hot enough to burn my skin, I step in and take the fastest shower of my life.

Still, after I dry off and step out in just a towel, my eyes flash to my empty bed.

Oh.

Well.

I guess that answers that.

I stressed over a conversation that isn't even going to happen.

I tighten my towel and then head for the kitchen.

The moment I turn the corner, I find Luca rummaging through the refrigerator. He pulls out the milk, eggs, and cheese. He closes the door, spots me, and smiles.

He's cute and shy as he sets everything on the counter and scratches his bare chest. Then, his eyes take in a painfully slow head-to-toe view of me.

Our eyes lock. He winks.

"I thought I could make you breakfast."

Oh my god.

I'm starting to think this man is too good to be true.

And why is he both so freaking cute and sexy at the same time?

It's annoying.

He's annoying.

And it's annoying how much I like him.

"What did you have in mind?" I ask and pull up a seat at the kitchen table. My house is small and doesn't have a kitchen island. It's just one big open room that lets me admire my personal chef of the day as he makes himself right at home.

It's one morning and I already know I could get used to this.

"A scramble of sorts."

"Of sorts," I repeat. "Do you want help?"

"No. I can cook."

"Another hidden talent."

"I'm not phenomenal or anything, but it won't make you sick, so it counts."

"Edible food is always nice."

"Are you going to have a remark for everything I say?"

"Of course. It's our thing."

He pauses to look over his shoulder. His eyes slowly roam my body. His perusal lingers on where my towel hits my thighs and every inch of his focus makes me squirm with need.

He moves toward.

"We have a thing?"

"We've always had a thing."

"What else do we have?" he asks, stopping right in front of me and crouching to meet me at eye level.

"We …" My sentence drifts when he puts a hand on each of my knees and gently spreads my legs. My brain instantly races as I remember that I'm wearing nothing but a towel.

"We what?"

His hand snakes up my inner thigh.

I let out a breath and shake my head. "You know I can't think when you touch me."

"Fair. How about I go first?"

His finger inches closer to my core, brushing against me.

"I have a thing for the way you look in just my shirt, but

right now, I'm pretty sure the way you look in nothing but a towel will be my favorite."

He slowly untucks my towel and starts to open it.

My eyes close as I inhale.

"I have a thing for the way you have to focus on each breath you take when I touch you."

He lowers his head and blows on me, right between the legs. My entire body jerks.

I reach up to thread my hands through his hair.

"I have a thing for when you moan. It's like a beacon to my cock. It tells me to kiss or lick every inch of your body until the moment you let me sink deep, deep inside you."

My next breath is like a stutter.

"And my newest thing is what I'm having for breakfast."

There is no time to think over what he's said. My legs open wider and he fills them, his tongue licking up my core to the clit.

He flicks it.

"Oh, Luca."

He pulls back only for a breath and then presses his entire face to where I want him most. He's kissing me and licking me, his tongue inside of me and commanding every cell of my body.

What would normally take longer sends me screaming his name in seconds.

"Luca!"

He doesn't slow. He doesn't even flinch at my cries. No, he moves faster, and just as my orgasm hits, he slides two fingers inside of me, curling them and circling my clit with his tongue as I black out.

When I come down from my high, he's watching me with fascination.

"I've never seen something so beautiful as you when you're falling apart from my mouth, Shay."

He kisses me hard. It's rough and passionate.

Then his arms swoop down to pick me up, wrapping my legs around his hips and walking us right back to my room.

He lowers me to the bed slowly.

"Let's see if I can do it again."

He doesn't say it in a cocky tone. He says it with determination. As if this is how it's supposed to be.

And maybe it is.

I just didn't know it until Luca.

I scoot to the middle of the bed, and Luca crawls over me the entire way, never letting his body leave mine.

It's the sexiest thing I've ever seen a man do.

When I stop, his lips are on mine as if he just can't hold himself back any longer.

Everything about this feels right.

His touch makes me feel lighter.

His kisses make me feel desirable.

I can't get over how calm being with Luca makes me.

It's mind-blowing, considering how much we bicker.

But even then, I love it.

"God, Shay, I can't get enough of you."

He kisses down my neck. I assume he's going to go for my bare chest next, but he doesn't. Instead he kisses down one arm, causing me to break out into laughter at how much it tickles.

He looks up at me with hungry eyes.

Then he moves to the other arm.

I giggle again.

"I fucking love that noise."

I roll my eyes.

His gaze instantly darkens as he grabs my chin to make me look at him.

It makes my heart race and the spot between my legs ache.

Sweet yet rough in bed.

I'll take it.

"Roll your eyes at me again and I'll have to punish you."

I smirk and then lift my hips.

"Punish me how?"

His eyes glow, and he blows out a breath.

"Maybe I want to be punished."

He lets out a growl.

So I push him further. "What happened to *whatever you want, baby it's yours*?"

"What do you want, Shay?"

"I want you. Right now."

"I was hoping you would say that."

He plants each hand on either side of my face to hold himself as he slides his body higher. His hips brush mine, causing me to open my legs wider. With his knees between mine, he runs his hands down my inner thighs, pushing them open even more.

In a moment where I think I should be vulnerable for being so on display for him, I'm anything but. Hell, it's early morning, the sun is shining bright into the room, and I'm just here for his viewing. I couldn't hide even if I wanted to.

"Look," Luca says, commanding my attention.

I follow his gaze to where our bodies touch. He's pulled

himself from his briefs, his hand slowly stroking the biggest cock I've ever seen.

Because of course it is.

Huge.

I knew it.

"You did this, Shay. You made this hard."

"Good," I snap back without a second thought.

His head falls back with a deep chuckle. Then he looks me in the eye.

"Let's see how well you take it."

I bite my lip as he leans over to grab his jeans from yesterday and pulls a condom out. He slips it over himself, and I let out a moan as I watch.

Then he slides the tip in, and I suck in breath.

"Breathe, Shay."

I do as I'm told as he slides in farther.

"That's it. You're doing so well."

As if he thinks I can't handle this. I don't think so.

I lift a leg, hooking it to his lower back, and then I push, making him sink all the way inside of me.

"Fuuuuuuck," he says, resting his head on mine as we both suck in a breath.

I kiss him as my response to how amazing it makes me feel.

My hands thread into his hair, and I grip tight.

He pulls out slowly and then slides back in just as slow.

Once. Twice. Three times he does this before he speeds up.

I can feel my orgasm coming quickly, and it's so sudden that I don't have time to warn him.

"I'm coming," I cry out.

He pushes up, his gaze dropping to where he's disappearing between my legs. Faster and faster he thrusts, encouraging my orgasm to keep going.

I can't think. I can't do anything but grab my own hair and tug as I let him own my entire body. He pulls one nipple into his mouth and then the other.

"Shit, shit," he says and then stills, letting out a low groan.

It isn't until his thumb brushes against my cheek that I realize my eyes are closed.

"Are you okay?" he asks when I look up at him.

I nod. "Better than okay."

And it's the truth.

Now, I just have to figure out how to never let this feeling go.

———

I walk into The Marina an hour later than usual that morning.

Grace is just pushing her breakfast plate away when I join her at the bar.

"Oh, look who it is," she teases. "I want to be shocked that you're late, but I know you and you know who have been working late on this place. I have to tell you, Shay, the dining room looks beautiful. I can't wait for the new tables and chairs to get here so you can open it up again. I also wanted to ask about the deck and why the side is now blocked off and… why are you looking at me like that?"

She points her finger at my face.

"Are you okay?"

I smile so big, my cheeks start to hurt.

"What? Oh my gosh what?"

"I …" I look around to see where Carl is. "Luca kissed me."

"Last night?"

I shake my head.

"Earlier this week, but again last night, and this morning after we woke up, we…" I scrunch my nose as I wait for the details to click into place with her.

Her eyes widen, and she slaps the countertop. "Yes. I knew it. Oh my gosh, finally. How was it? Good? I bet it was good."

"It was." I let out a sigh. "I'm ruined Grace. Ruined."

"Ruined. God, I hope I can refer to sex that way someday."

"I'm in this whole different world with him. I don't worry about anything, and I just get to be me. I mean, Grace, the ideas he has for this place are so good. I finally found someone who believes in it as much as I do, and it's a really nice feeling."

"Hey, I believe in it."

"You know what I mean. He's here and helping me and adding to my ideas, and it's like I have a little team that motivates me, and then when we aren't working we are ... well. I can't believe this is my life right now."

"I love this for you."

"I'd love it more if I didn't have to keep everything a secret."

"So don't."

"You know I can't do that."

"Well, you could," she says and gives me that look. You know, the one that says I control my life and can do whatever I want because I'm a grown-up.

Nowhere does it say that I own The Marina, though, because I don't, and until I do, I can't risk my parents selling it to someone else.

"Good morning." Linc Collins strolls into the room as if it's an everyday occurrence. He looks at Grace's breakfast plate. "I should start coming here for breakfast more often. I forget how stunning the view is."

We all glance out the back window, and while they are enjoying the landscape, I'm trying to run through any positive reason Linc would be here in his work attire with his work bag slung over his shoulder.

I want to demand he leave, because his presence can't mean anything good, but he's only here to do his job, and I can't fault him for that.

"What brings you in today?" I ask as calmly as I can.

He has no expression on his face when he says, "I'm getting pictures for your parents."

"Pictures?" I repeat.

"They still haven't confirmed if they want to sell, but they want to be ready."

I can't believe this.

My parents have called Linc more than they have me in the last three weeks. I should be the one they share this information with first.

A heads-up would be nice.

"Sure. Make sure you get pictures of this dining room. It's freshly remodeled."

I stand with jerky movements and take my place behind the bar and cross my arms.

"If you want good pictures of the main hallway, come

back next week when I'm finished painting them. If you want a picture of the cabins, that will be another month."

"Shay," Grace says softly.

"I know you're just doing your job, Linc, but this is … wrong."

He nods and takes a step back.

"I'll tell them my schedule is busy this week."

"And next," I say with more snap than I want. So I take it down a notch when I add on, "Please."

He nods and then waves goodbye as he leaves.

"That was unexpected," Grace says slowly.

"How could my parents do this? Why wouldn't they call me first?"

"You heard him, Shay. They haven't decided yet."

"They keep calling him, Grace. That's basically saying that their minds are made up and the only reason they haven't signed the dotted line is because they said I had till the end of the summer."

"Which is still six weeks away."

I glance out the window at where we used to hold live bands and grill food and people would be having so much fun that we had to ask them to leave well after closing.

The indoors might not be fully accessible yet, but the beach is always ready.

It's time to buckle down and be smart.

The Marina needs my full focus.

I can't be caught doing anything that could cause my parents to change their minds sooner than later.

I just hope that chance will still be there when the summer is over.

CHAPTER SIXTEEN

LUCA

I think about two things for the remainder of my day.

First, this thing with Shay has made me happier than I've been in a long time. Second, the fact that I can't tell a single soul about my feelings for her sucks.

It reminds me of the summer Ruby got pregnant. I'd been hanging out with a girl who I knew was only here for the summer. I was young and looking for fun. I knew it wouldn't turn into anything serious, but that doesn't mean how it ended hurt any less.

Me and this girl had been hooking up day after day, sometimes twice a day. Then I saw her on the beach one day with her family and when I went to say hi, like a nice normal guy would, she pretended she didn't know me.

Later, she asked if we could still sneak around in secret.

I clearly wasn't good enough for her rich family. Which, whatever, fine, but be upfront about it.

That was basically the summer I banned tourists from

fling status and decided that being honest was the only way to go.

But it's different this time. I'm an adult who went into this knowing that working with Shay was a secret, but still, how long will this need to last?

I do a quick midday check in with my guys then head to Hudson's for lunch. As soon as I walk in the door, I spot Miles and Quinn sitting at the bar, completely caught up in their own little bubble, their relationship on full display for the world to see.

I'm happy for him, but it stings.

I take a deep breath and move to join them, but I spot Declan on the other side of the bar, solo.

His vibe fits my current mood more, so I head in his direction instead.

"Everything okay?"

I nod.

"Oooh, a nod for a reply. What's up?"

"Nothing," I say and pull out my phone to text Shay.

LUCA

How's your day going?

THEN I FLIP it face down on the counter. Maybe if I just have some sort of communication with her during the day, even if I can't see her, I'll stop obsessing over this.

"Luca," Declan repeats my name.

"Yeah?"

"Are you sure you're okay?"

I nod again. "It's been a long day in the sun."

"I hear that. I've been playing outside with Susie all morning, and I think I got a little sunburnt."

He taps his nose.

"Where is Susie?" I ask.

"Her mom is in town for the night, so they are staying at the lodge."

"Oh, a free man tonight?" I joke.

"More like get shit done and catch up on sleep kind of night."

"Productive. I like it."

"The usual?" Hudson asks, appearing out of nowhere.

"Yep."

Then, as if we planned it, Miles takes a seat next to me, Dutton walks in the door, and Linc walks in from the bookstore.

In just minutes, we are all seated together.

"What happened to Quinn?"

"She was meeting up with Sadie."

"Cool."

"Today is a weird day," Linc says.

"Not as weird as my day," Dutton chimes in. "Any chance any of you know how to get a woman to say yes to something without having to do something in—"

"No," we all say without hearing the rest of his questions.

He chuckles.

"Noted."

"What happened to you?" I ask Linc.

This is good. If I focus on the problems of those around

me, I can't dwell on the idea that I'm only good enough as a secret.

Shit, did I really just think that?

"It's just that selling things in town when families you know are involved can be tricky."

"Are you talking about The Marina?" Declan asks.

"Who said The Marina was for sale?" I ask quickly. Shay has shared some things with me, but as far as she knows, it's not for sale yet. Unless this is the tricky part Linc is referring to.

"It's not—technically. I shouldn't be talking about this with you guys."

"I want to know. That place is part of this town, and the Parkers have owned it for three decades. They can't sell it."

Linc winces. "They can if that's what they decide."

"Then Shay can buy it."

"I heard it was losing money and they won't sell it to her."

My attention snaps to Dutton.

He starts placing his lunch order with Hudson.

I would question him, but he is the brother of Shay's best friend. If anyone were to know something about The Marina that was true, it would be him.

"I hate small-town rumors," I murmur and get a collective response of agreement. "And it's not fair to Shay that we are talking about her without her here, so let's not."

"It's hard not to get caught up," Dutton says. "We hear everything at the lodge. It's just part of the town at this point."

The rest of our lunch goes quietly. Well, quietly on the outside. My mind is racing with thoughts of Shay and the fate of The Marina. She has so much to worry about these days that my complaining over why I can't tell people about us seems like it can wait.

Still, as I walk out of the bar and back to work, I glance down at my phone.

Still no response.

It's fine.

It is. She doesn't have to text me back if she doesn't want to. Like I said, she's busy.

But fuck it, it's going to drive me crazy until I see her tonight.

It hasn't even been twelve hours and I'm counting down the minutes until I can see her again.

Text or no text, busy or not, I can only hope that she's doing the same thing.

———

As soon as I pull up to The Marina, I let out a breath. The parking lot is still busy. But to be fair, I am early.

Perhaps she hasn't replied because she's simply just that, busy. I glance at the door, trying to tell myself that I don't need to go inside and demand that she talk to me. I don't wanna be that kind of guy, but fuck if I can't get that woman off my mind. All day every day since our first kiss she's all I think about. Did she sleep well? How was her breakfast? Does she want to have breakfast with me again, breakfast the way we had it this morning? Can I sneak over and see her in the middle of the day? I just want her around me all the time. It's driving me absolutely mad that she hasn't returned my message.

The door opens, and there she is. Her gaze swings to my

truck, and her eyes widen. She ducks right back into The Marina, closing the door.

Oh hell no. I refuse to let things between us go back to the way they were. Ever.

I get out of my truck and march straight for the front door.

Shay doesn't even try to hide as she stands behind the bar pouring a beer and pretending as if she had no idea I was here.

"Luca, how's it going?"

She smiles at the customer who ordered the beer then acts as if there is an extra dirty spot on the counter in front of her.

"How's it going?" I say with a sarcastic tone. "How's it *going*?"

She doesn't even fake her smile. It's completely real.

"Yes. How's it going? "

I glance around the room to make sure we're alone, because fuck all if I still want to respect her wishes that no one knows about us in a moment when I need her to need me as much I need her.

Jesus. Listen to me. I'm obsessed with her.

"Well, to be honest, Shay, I would be a whole lot better if the girl I was crushing on would message me back," I say slowly so there's no way for her to ask me to repeat myself. I was very clear. Minus maybe the part where the girl is her, but she's smart enough to figure it out.

"Oh." She glances outside the large marina windows toward the lake and then back at me. "Perhaps this girl is just a little busy and not sure what to think about things right now."

So that's where her mind is.

Taking my frustration down a notch, I say, "Well I wish

she knew she could come and talk to me about it. Because I like her. Like a stupid amount."

She smirks and then bites her bottom lip.

The urge to tell her that's *my* bottom lip hits me hard, but I don't. I'll save that for later.

"I'll be sure to pass the message along," she says with a grin.

"You do that."

"Until then," she says before I have time to obsess over whether I need to leave now or not, "Turns out that cabin three needs new upper cabinets in the kitchen nook. Can you go look at it before you leave, for measurements?"

Work. She wants to just cut straight to work?

Maybe that's what she needs me to do. Reassure her that no matter what happens, I promise not to let it affect my work here.

"I'm on it," I say and turn for the door.

It takes everything I have inside myself not to reach for her and kiss her goodbye.

I want that.

But I don't want to rush her either.

I walk out the door, wave to a couple of locals who are friends with my dad, then grab my tool bag from the back of my truck. I check to make sure a few key pieces are inside the bag before I make the walk to cabin three.

I don't remember the cabinets in any of them needing to be fully replaced, but my mind was a little elsewhere the day we looked at them.

The light is on when I get there, which makes sense since Shay was clearly in here earlier.

I walk in and there is no stopping the grin that forms on my lips.

"Hi." Shay blushes and stands from where she's been sitting at the kitchen table waiting for me.

I drop my tool bag to the floor. "Hi."

Her hands fidget in front of her as she walks toward me.

"I don't know how to do this."

"Do what?"

"This." She waves a hand between us. "I just know that you love honesty, and I need to give you that."

"Okay."

"Obviously, I like you, too."

I smirk.

She rolls her eyes.

"But it doesn't change the fact that people can't know you're remodeling this place, and if they can't know that, then they definitely can't know we're sleeping together."

I nod slowly.

It still sucks to hear.

"Remind me why people can't know that you hired me. Is it only because your family doesn't like me?"

She breaks eye contact instantly and hesitates to answer.

In fact, she takes so long that I almost tell her she doesn't have to tell me. I don't want to make her uncomfortable.

"When I came back and took over, my parents told me that I could turn this place around as long as I didn't hire you."

Shit.

Her family really has zero trust left in me.

"And what happens if they find out you did?"

She shrugs quickly.

"I don't want to find out."

Then she does that thing where she looks everywhere but at me, her eyes bouncing like a fucking pinball machine that's ready to break.

She's not telling me something. I'm not saying what she just admitted isn't true, because it sounds on track with everything we have been through, but she's holding back details.

They must be bad ones.

She shifts on her feet, and I hate putting her in this spot. One where she clearly has to choose between what she wants with me and what she wants to make her family happy.

I'll never be that guy who has to make her choose.

No one is going to die, so whatever she's keeping can't be that bad.

I reach for her, pulling her into my arms. Once I have her wrapped up tight against my chest, I feel her entire body relax.

"You won't have to."

And she won't. Not if I get a say in the matter.

———

I SPEND the next couple of hours working in one of the cabins while Shay finishes her day at The Marina.

The moon is shining over the lake, giving a calm presence to the cabin when Shay walks back in.

"Should we get back to it in the main building?"

I nod, eager to follow and spend time with her.

Now, I know I have to work when we get there, but I'm hoping to steal a kiss or two as well. I've never been this into anyone I've dated. So into them that even being apart for a few hours feels like I'm missing something.

Of course, there is no way I'm going to admit this to her right now. My feelings for her went from zero to one hundred real quick, and I don't want to freak her out if she doesn't feel the same way.

"How many colors are you planning to use in this building?" I ask, keeping to the task at hand as best I can.

We step through the main doors, and the moonlight lights up the room, casting the perfect streak of light over Shay's sun-kissed face as she smiles over her shoulder at me.

"Do you want to see my Pinterest board of ideas?"

I nod. "Yep."

She grabs my hand and pulls me to one of the three couches that line the room. The couches are the only things in here that she didn't replace. With the big windows, it makes sense to have seating areas aside from formal dining, but I see why she wanted to remodel the space so that those sitting in the couches and those eating dinner could enjoy two different experiences without being right on top of each other.

Once I sit, she pulls her knees up and lets them fall over my thigh as she settles right next to me.

"Okay, so I was thinking about these colors."

Her phone shines back at me with blues, greens, and golds.

"Then I think we could add in bits of soft coral, too."

She swipes through a few more photos, going on and on about how the coral pillows in this room will be enough and how she's already got the blue in the hallways and wants to add more plants for the earthy vibe but hasn't quite figured out the coral or gold for that space yet.

"What if you take pictures from the past years here with

your family, make them black-and- white, and then alter frames in the coral and gold?"

She slowly looks at me, her lips tugging into a smile.

"I think that would be perfect."

"You could even have a couple of empty ones to fill as the years go on."

Her lips part on a breath.

My heart immediately beats faster. I reach for her, one hand on her legs, the other sneaking around her back as I lean into her.

"Luca," she breathes my name on a sigh. "We still have work to do tonight."

"Well, then, you need to stop what you're doing."

She slides a hand into my hair, curls her fingers, and tugs gently just as my lips press to her neck.

"And what am I doing?"

I kiss her neck once more, then her cheek as I whisper into her ear, "You're tempting me."

"Am I now?"

"Mm-hmm."

"What are you going to do about it?"

I move fast, hands on her hips as I pull her fully into my lap, her legs resting on either side of me.

"I'm going to kiss you for a good five minutes at least, then I'm going to get to work, because if I don't, I'm going to get so lost in you that I won't be able to focus on anything else."

"And you're okay with stopping to work?"

"I am."

"Oh."

Her voice is low and her head dips, so I gently touch her chin and force her to look at me.

"If you're thinking it's because I don't want you, you're wrong. It's because this marina means a lot to you and you mean a lot to me, so we are doing this. And then, I'm doing you."

She erupts into laughter, grabs my face, and kisses me hard.

"Let's just get to work now. The sooner we finish means the sooner we—"

"Finish," I say, completing her sentence.

She giggles and climbs off my lap to stand.

"Okay, cheeseball, let's go."

I stand and pull her in for one more kiss.

A guy sure could get used to nights like this, and seeing as how for right now, this is all I get, I plan to.

CHAPTER SEVENTEEN

SHAY

Two nights later, I head into town with a stack of flyers in my hand.

The flyers Luca and I made last night before he spent another night at my house. That's three nights in a row now. If I'm not careful, I'm not going to want to go back to nights without him.

I honestly can't remember a time when I was this happy. This content.

I'd do anything to keep it, which is why I'm not going home until I've handed out every single one of these.

The closer I get to the heart of Main Street, the more I make out who's attending today's town festival. I'm not surprised when I see Mrs. Whittaker first. Her family has been around the longest, and seeing as how today is the 100 Years of Lovers Festival, it makes sense that she is here.

Next, I see the Collins family. Mr. Collins, Linc, and Sadie are standing under a tent that is serving beers from Hudson's Bar. Beside them is Brooke under her bakery tent.

"Shay," Sadie calls out.

Her brother and her dad both turn to face me and smile with a wave. Well, her dad does. Linc excuses himself quickly.

I don't blame him.

I was snappy the other day when he came to take pictures. I'll have to find him later and apologize.

"The festival started a half hour ago, so why does it look like everyone has been here all day?"

"Because some of them have." Sadie laughs as she pours a beer from the keg to hand to a tourist.

I swear, they love coming back to this town again and again because of the festivals. During the summer, there is one almost every weekend.

In fact, there is a festival every weekend over the summer, except for the weekend I picked for The Marina opening, which is why I chose it.

"Can you hand some of these out?" I ask and hold up a small stack of flyers.

"Beach Bum Day," Sadie reads, and a big smile forms on her lips. "Does this mean The Marina is ready for its big reveal?"

"No," I say with a little laugh. "It's close, but not ready. All of this will be outside on the beach. Music, food, drinks, games. It'll be fun."

"With as hot as it has been this summer, I'd say people are going to love a reason to be next to the water."

"I hope so."

"I'll hand them out with the drinks until they're gone."

"Thank you."

Another customer comes up, so I wave goodbye and spot Grace heading my way.

She's still in business attire, but today is a pencil skirt and a sleeveless cream blouse. I've known her long enough to know that the skirt comes with a matching jacket, but it's understandable why she isn't wearing it.

"I didn't think you were coming," I say when she stops in front of me.

"The entire Richford family is here," she says with no emotion. "Plus the King family."

"Oooh." I cringe for her.

The King family is the family who probably visits Lovers the most. They are basically honorary locals at this point, but they have a son—a full adult, mind you—who Grace has never been able to get along with. Not since day one.

In fact, she refers to him as his royal dumbass, and I love it. I used to think I needed to give Luca a nickname, but I never got around to it. It's probably a good thing now that I'm sleeping with him.

"Shit, they see me. I have to go."

Grace doesn't wait for my reply before she walks off quickly.

Preston King, also known as his royal dumbass, strides past me, his light gray suit sharp and with a grin that should be on magazines. Which is funny to think about since he has actually been in magazines.

I think the last one called him bachelor of the year or something.

I watch him walk down the street in Grace's direction. Is he looking for her specifically?

"Like what you see?" A deep voice startles me.

When I look to my left to match the voice with a face, I keep my expression neutral.

"Maybe."

Luca hums. "Maybe, huh?"

It takes everything I have not to smile at the look he gives me. To fall into his arms and relax under his touch. But then his gaze flickers to my lips, and I step back.

"Whatever you're thinking, stop," I say and point a finger at him. To anyone watching, that gesture should come off as me telling him off.

His head falls back on a groan.

He looks agitated.

"I'll see you tonight," I whisper and walk off.

When I glance over my shoulder, his eyes are on me, and I swear just knowing he's watching me wakes my body up.

Now is not the time for me to be turned on.

My phone beeps.

LUCA

Meet me in the bookstore in ten minutes.

SHAY

That's a very public spot.

LUCA

I know a back room.

My heart races at the idea of sneaking around. We're already doing it, but here in town, it would be different. Riskier.

SHAY

Okay.

I stuff my phone into my back pocket and get to work

handing out flyers. According to the feedback I receive, the locals are eager to be back at The Marina, and as I head for the bookstore, my heart is full with the excitement of Beach Bum Day. Now I just need to make sure it's so successful that everyone is talking about it and word somehow gets back to my parents.

I open the door to Sips and Stories, welcoming the breeze from the air conditioner. I glance around to make sure no one is here, then slowly make my way to the back of the store. The wall that opens up to the bar shows very few customers.

None of them are paying attention to me.

I walk down one aisle and peek around to spot Luca, but he isn't here yet.

My palms start to sweat.

Am I here just so he can steal a kiss?

More than a kiss?

Surely, he doesn't think we are going to full on have sex in a back room somewhere, right?

I'm starting to second-guess this plan when a hand grabs my wrist and pulls me back. Tucked in a nook, Luca hugs my body to his and kisses my neck.

"It's one thing when I know you're at The Marina and I won't see you until dark, but it's a whole different thing to see you this close in broad daylight and know I can't do a single thing about it."

He nips kisses over my shoulder, and it feels so good. Having this moment with him is unexpected and exactly what I needed.

I wish we could see each other whenever we want, too, but it can't happen yet.

"It sure seems like you're doing something about it." My

words are breathless as he smooths one hand down my stomach, his pinky sliding under the waist of my shorts. "Luca."

"God, the way you say my name drives me crazy. You sound so needy. I love it."

He spins me quickly, then his lips are on mine. His tongue slips into my mouth, dancing with mine. I grip his shirt and pull his body closer to mine on a moan.

The sounds of Main Street grow louder, a clear indicator that someone has opened the door to the bookstore.

I break the kiss, my chest heaving as I quietly catch my breath. Luca turns us so that my back is against the wall and his body blocks me from anyone's view.

He rests his forehead against mine as we wait to be sure that whoever walked in doesn't walk this far inside the store.

My heart thumps.

Who is it?

Is it someone we could trust?

Then I hear that street noise again, just long enough to indicate that whoever it was has left. I push Luca back.

"That was risky."

He nods, his hand moving to rub the back of his neck.

I know exactly what he's thinking before he even says it.

"I will tell them," I admit. "I just don't want to do it over the phone, and I don't want them to hear it from someone else before I have time to explain."

"I know. I just hate hiding how I feel about you. Hiding this. It sucks."

"I know, but it won't be forever," I tell him and hope it's enough for now.

He leans back to peek into the store. He must deem it clear —he grabs my hand and pulls me out the back door.

Behind the building is a small alley that has a back entrance to every business on this side of the block, including where Sadie and Hudson live above the bar.

Luca leads me to the door to their place and ducks inside.

I follow and he pulls me in for another kiss.

"I just need another minute with you before I have to pretend like we aren't even friends for the rest of the afternoon."

He kisses me with so much passion that I have the urge to say *fuck it*. I'm a grown woman. Who cares if word gets back to my family?

But … I do.

Until The Marina is in my name, I do.

For the next ten minutes, Luca and I make out like teenagers who don't want to get caught by the faculty at a Friday night football game.

Then we go our separate ways back to the festival.

For the rest of the afternoon, I tell everyone I meet about Beach Bum Day, and each time I pass Luca or see him nearby, I wish it were dark already so that I could touch him again.

It's only for the summer.

After that, I can touch him anywhere and anytime, right?

CHAPTER EIGHTEEN

LUCA

I misjudged my self-control when it came to Shay.

For the last two weeks, it's taken everything I have inside me not to grab her when I see her in line at B's Bakery and kiss her, or to pull her into a quiet corner when I catch her walking down Main Street, or to show up a girls' night and whisk her away because I want more time with her. I crave more time with her. Every night, we work for a few hours, then either we can't wait a moment longer and start stripping right there in The Marina or we rush back to her place. But that's not enough for me.

I want all her moments.

I want every moment of the day with her.

I'm so completely screwed.

As soon as my family and I hit the sand and set out chairs with a few other items to settle in for an afternoon in the sun, other locals started to trickle in.

It's Beach Bum Day and nearing a hundred degrees

outside. Being in the water sounds like a wonderful way to cool off.

But more people also means keeping my hands off Shay. Watching her play and laugh with my family and then mingle with everyone else, completely in her element ... I'm both proud and I hate every moment of it, because I want to be right next to her. Sharing this with her.

I walk back to where Ruby and Max set up an umbrella and some loungers and take a seat, digging into the cooler next to me to grab a beer.

I don't plan on going back to my house tonight, and Shay's house is a quick walk from here.

I pop the top and take a sip just as Hudson sits down next to me.

I can see him watching me out of the corner of my eye.

"So," he starts. I wait for him to say more, but he just chuckles as if that explains it all.

"So," I repeat.

His laugh intensifies.

"No, you don't get to be the I-told-you-so guy right now," I whisper snap at him. "Fifteen months ago, you wouldn't have even been at breakfast. So if anyone gets to be that guy, it's me."

He laughs harder.

"Stop."

"I can't help it."

"You're a grown man. You can totally help it."

His laughter quiets, but the smile remains. "I just ... I like this side of you, and I'm glad you finally caved."

"Right, yes, because you're Mr. Know-It-All about romance now."

Between Shay spending time with Sadie and me showing up every day at lunch at Hudson's, it was easy for him to put things together. I actually think most of my family knows, but I haven't exactly announced it. Seeing as how Shay doesn't want people to know, I appreciate that my brother figured it out and I have someone to talk to about this.

Hudson grabs a beer and volleys his head.

"More than you for … what did you say, fifteen months now?"

I let out a sigh, but then I hear Shay and the girls laughing, and I have no choice but to smile.

That's my favorite sound.

"I told you," Hudson says.

I'm opening my mouth to argue a little more, but he holds up his hand.

"I told you that when it hits, it hits hard, didn't I?"

I glance back out over the view in front of us. The girls are playing tag with Max and Susie.

Max tries to run by Shay, but she reaches out and grabs him, spinning him with his feet off the ground. When she sets him down, both he and Susie grab Shay's hands, pulling her into the water. Quickly, Sadie and Ruby join in until Shay goes under. She pops up with a smile on her face, pulling Max down into the water with her.

Hudson's not wrong.

I'm so far gone for this girl, I can't think of a moment in my life that I don't want to share with her.

I just wish that she was ready to be in this spot with me.

I don't need us to be at this speed to know she wants to be with me, too, but it would be nice.

"Yeah, you were right." I say and take a swig of my beer.

Declan plops down onto the sand on the other side of me, so I hand him a beer.

"I haven't seen Susie this happy since we moved back," he admits. "I really appreciate your family inviting us to tag along today."

"Anytime," Hudson says at the same time I say, "Why is my sister always pissed off at you?"

Declan groans. "When you find out, let me know."

To that I grin. Ruby may have been gone for a few years, but she's got that grumpy Asher blood in her veins just as much as the rest of us.

"Has Shay told her family about you two yet?"

I glance at my brother. I have a long answer for everything, but right now, I give him the short one.

I shake my head.

"Is she planning on it?"

"Yeah, of course. She just wants to wait, and do it face-to-face when they are back."

"When is that?"

"Two weeks from tomorrow."

Yeah, yeah, so what if I'm counting down the days for the moment I can finally walk down Main Street with her hand in mine?

I'm gone for this woman. I want everyone to know it.

"That's not too bad."

"Can't people see you now?" Declan asks. "I mean, even I know something is going on and I don't talk to you every single day. I just live here."

I nod. "I think just our friends and my family have caught on."

He shakes his head, and I don't need to look him in the eyes to know what he's thinking.

I take a breath and blow it out slowly.

People do silly things when they fall in love.

And I fell hard.

"I'm just going to run inside for more water," Shay calls as she passes us.

"Need help?" Declan asks.

"Nope," she answers quickly and keeps walking.

One.

Two.

Three.

Four.

Whelp, that should be enough time.

I stand quickly, the sound of my brother whispering "I knew it" to Declan behind me as I make my way to The Marina right behind Shay.

I watch as she steps into the back employee entrance.

I do exactly the same.

Shay is the only one in the room, so I close the door quietly and then tiptoe my way to her.

She glances up, and her eyes widen.

"What are you doing?"

"What do you think I'm doing?"

"I think you're trying to get caught."

She looks around quickly and then grabs me by the shirt, pulling me into a nearby closet.

"Ah, who's trying to be sneaky now," I tease.

She rolls her eyes and then locks her arms around my neck as she kisses me.

She doesn't even try to give the illusion that she wants

something soft and sweet. No, Shay kisses me with hunger, and the moment her tongue slips into my mouth, stroking with my own, I back her up to the wall.

"How far can I get right now?"

"All the way," she says without thinking it over.

Luckily, she's in her swimsuit with a teal skirt cover-up, and I'm in nothing but a pair of swim trunks.

"There isn't much room for me to make this romantic," I point out.

"I know."

"Do you want—"

"Just fuck me, Luca. It's simple."

Her eyes widen. She's no doubt shocked that those words came from her lips and not mine.

Her lips form a little "o" as she waits for my response.

Which is to give her exactly as she wants.

I spin her around and then jerk her swim bottoms down to her knees. I run my hand from the top of her ass and up her back, gently forcing her to lean forward.

"Find something to hold on to, and don't make a sound."

She looks over her shoulder and bites her lip, nodding.

With her ass on display for me, I untie my shorts and pull my hardened cock out, running the tip along her slit.

"Fuck," I say, dragging the word out.

"You wanted me to follow you, didn't you?" I ask her.

"I was hoping you would, yes."

I push the head inside another inch then lean forward, my mouth right against her ear. "If you want my cock, Shay, all you have to do is ask for it."

"I want your cock," she says without missing a beat. "Please."

Please. I swear I grow even harder. Like my dick knows she's begging for him.

I slide in a little more, her moan filling the silence of the empty closet.

"Shh." I wrap a hand around her mouth to quiet the noises she makes. "You don't want to get caught, do you?"

At that, my cock slides in deeper.

"Jesus, does the idea of someone seeing you like this make you wetter?"

She nods lightly.

"Oh, she has a kink. I like it," I say, then slam into her, filling her completely.

She bites down on my hand when I'm as deep as I can go, so I pull back and slam into her again.

And again.

And again.

When I feel her walls clamping down on me, I pick up my pace. I remove my hand from her mouth to hold her hips steady.

"Oh fuck," she whimpers. "I'm there. I'm right there."

I reach around, my index and middle finger rubbing small circles on her clit until she shatters.

"Luca, yes, oh my god."

Her hand slaps the wall in front of her.

Her pussy tightens throughout her climax, ripping my own from my body in seconds. I pull out and stroke myself over and over as I come all over her lower back.

I catch my breath as I wrap an arm around her hips to help her stand. Then I grab a napkin off one of the shelves, clean off her back, and help her get dressed again. All the while, she's tucking me back into my shorts.

As soon as she's done with the tie at my waistband, my cock jumps, ready to go again.

Shay slowly opens the door.

When the coast is clear, she leads me out the back door.

"We've made a lot of memories here," I say. "But that might be my favorite one."

Shay rolls her eyes and then winks at me.

"Are you staying over tonight?"

"Yes."

"Good."

And then she walks off while I wait back in the trees so no one sees us together.

When I suspect Shay is out of sight, I make my way back to where Hudson and Declan are still sitting.

I take back my seat and grab a new beer.

"So, ah," Declan clears his throat. "Where are the waters?"

Shit.

CHAPTER NINETEEN

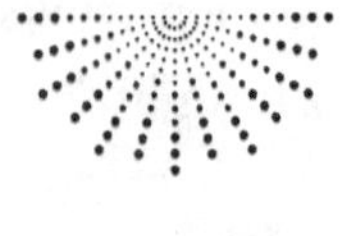

SHAY

It's girls' night, and I already know they are going to tease me about Luca.

Not only because I fought it for so long when they told me something was there, but because I missed the last girls' night by staying in his bed.

I walk inside Brooke's house without calling out a greeting.

As soon as I spot everyone in the kitchen, Grace starts laughing and Sadie rushes to hug me.

"Yay! You're here."

"I'm here."

Quinn pokes her head from around the kitchen and smiles.

"How's your day?" she asks.

Quinn hasn't been to that many girls' nights, but I have chatted with her around town in the past month.

"Good," I answer, and Grace pops out from behind Quinn.

"I know that tone. What happened?"

I let out a sigh and think about my afternoon.

The afternoon that I told not a single soul about.

"I went by the bank today."

The bank was always a plan B for me. If my parents wouldn't sell to me, I'd get the loan and try to buy it as if I were any other customer.

But turns out, I can't afford to buy The Marina on my own.

Part of me thinks that's why I hadn't gone that route yet. I knew I wouldn't get approved, but after the last few weeks with Luca, I was feeling motivated, like I could do anything.

Anything but buy The Marina, that is.

My only chance now is that my parents finally do decide to sell to me and we work out some kind of deal. A buyout of sorts.

I don't know.

I don't really know how to make this work anymore. I just know that I don't see myself doing anything else in life. My degree could let me start up any other business, but that's not what I imagined for myself. It was always me and The Marina, and now, it's me, The Marina, and Luca.

But for the first time, I'm realizing this might not actually be my future.

Instantly, all the girls appear in the living room. Grace, Quinn, Sadie, Brooke, and Ruby.

"And?" Brooke asks.

The tears start.

A part of me thought that if I could just get this loan, not only would I have this whole marina thing in the bag, but then I could stop sneaking around with Luca.

It wouldn't matter anymore if my family knew.

Still, until it was in my name … ugh, this all so stupid.

I'm a mess.

Maybe if I just knew what happened, all the real details, I could somehow fix things between our families.

I'd have to find a way that wasn't obvious as to why I was doing it, but I could.

I feel like so much of my life is out of my control. Either I'm about to snap or it's all going to fall apart.

"I'm so sorry, Shay. Can I do anything?" Grace asks.

"No. I'll be fine. I'll figure it out."

"Does Luca know you went to the bank?" Sadie asks. She's picking at the rim of her drink instead of looking at me.

"No. I … I thought … I don't know what I thought, but no, and I don't want him to know."

I don't think he would judge me, but I want him to be proud of me, and how can he do that if I'm not even proud of myself right now?

"Ugh. Let's talk about something else. I'm getting all sad, and I don't want that."

"Okay, so then let's talk about Sadie's bachelorette party," Brooke says, knowing the perfect topic to turn to.

"I'm not getting married until next summer," Sadie reminds her.

"So, it's never too early to start planning."

And that's what we do for the rest of the night. Before I know it, girls' night comes to an end.

We exchange hugs, and I'm just about to walk out the door when it opens and Hudson steps in, followed by Miles. They both greet their girls, and my heart swoons. Is this what it could be like if I just sucked it up? I mean what's the worst that could happen?

Your family might make you choose between The Marina and Luca.

Right. That.

"Good night," I call out.

Everyone sends me off with their version of goodbye, but it's Miles's words that stop me.

"Don't panic when you step out that door, Shay."

Then he winks at me.

I can't help it, I grin like a fool and walk outside.

It's dark, the moon the only bit of light, but it's just enough for me to spot the man standing at the end of the driveway next door.

He looks up and grins when he spots me practically skipping toward him.

"I figure it's dark out and people can't s—"

That's all he gets out before my lips are on his. His hands slink around my lower back, and he dips me back to kiss me with more passion.

"It's perfect."

I give him one more quick peck.

"Can I stay with you tonight?"

He nods quickly.

"Yep."

Hand in hand, we head for his house, only to come to an abrupt stop at the end of the street. It's dark out, and most people are in their homes in the evening. So seeing Mrs. Whittaker out walking her dog all by herself startles me.

I jump with a squeak and then take one step behind Luca. I'm not fully hidden, but I move enough to hide our laced fingers.

Or so I think.

Mrs. Whittaker's gaze snaps right to them, and she smirks.

"Evening," she says.

"Good evening, Mrs. W," Luca says in his everyday charming voice. "Lovely night for a walk."

"Yes," she says, looking back and forth between us. "It's a very good night."

She nods to me, and I return the gesture, hoping that will be the end of it and her age will mean she forgets this interaction all together by morning.

She resumes her walk, and I let out a breath. We did—

"I'm so happy you two are bringing That Marina back to life. I've missed that place," she says quickly.

I suck in breath and Luca chuckles, whispering in my ear, "I told you people would know."

I swat his arm, but Mrs. Whittaker doesn't stop to say more.

"If she knows, more people know," I say. "Which means my family will know soon."

"Not exactly," Luca says and pulls me toward his house. "She's clearly known for a while and hasn't said a word. In fact, no one has said anything about us to me or anyone I know. I think they respect the fact that we don't want people to know and they are pretending not to know."

I swallow and nod, but what if he's wrong?

I'm crossing my fingers that he's right, though.

"Do you think she'll tell people about this?" I ask and hold up our hands.

Luca takes a deep breath. "We won't know for sure, but my gut tells me that she's on our side and waiting for us to do things on our terms."

I nod, because the only thing I can control from here is praying that he's right.

My thoughts don't have time to get carried away because as soon as we get through the front door to Luca's house, he promptly removes all my clothes before we can make it up the stairs to his bed.

A girl could get used to this.

———

"Can I ask you something?" I say, rolling to my side and lifting a leg to rest over him as I snuggle him closer. I don't think there will ever be a right time to ask him this, so I need to just blurt it out.

"Oh boy, by the way you're biting your lip and staring out the window, I have a feeling I know what you want to ask me."

I try not to smile. "Do you?"

I reach up to cup his cheek and hold my hand there until he looks down at me.

"Yeah. Ask it."

"Why did you steal the money?"

He takes a deep breath, his gaze never leaving mine. In fact, I'm so lost in his eyes and how sad they look that I don't realize how long it takes him to answer.

"Is it that bad?" I whisper.

He pulls my hand away from his face then scoots down the bed until we are nose to nose.

"I never stole that money, Shay. I swear."

It's the same answer he gave us thirteen years ago, but this time, now that I know him better, I have zero doubt that he's telling the truth, and my heart hurts that none of us believed him before. That for as close as our families were back then, we didn't even give him a chance to explain. He deserved better from us. He deserved better from me.

"I believe you."

He lets out a breath, and I swear I see years of relief leave his body.

"You do?"

"I do."

"You didn't back then."

"I was young and dumb back then and didn't make my own opinion. I am now, and if you say you didn't steal the money, I believe you."

If I was going to say more, Luca doesn't let me.

His mouth is on mine with his next breath, and he's shifting our bodies until he's on top of me. He nudges my knees apart with one of his own, and I obey happily. When he settles himself against me, his hardened cock presses to my naked center. He pushes the tip inside teasingly.

"Luca." His name comes out breathlessly. "Please don't tease me."

"No?"

His lips move to my cheek, to my jaw, then he squeezes my breasts as he bites my ear.

"I don't mean to tease, Shay, but your body is so fucking responsive, I crave seeing your reactions to my touch. I'm addicted to it."

"I'm addicted to your cock, so please give it to me."

His deep chuckle only turns me on more. I lift my hips, my back bowing as I take another inch of him.

"Oh, my girl is greedy."

He grips my hips and then flips us so that he's on his back and I'm straddling his body.

"You want my body, Shay. Take it. Ride me. Fuck me the way you want it until your pussy clenches around my cock, and then I'll fuck you the way I want and make you come again."

Holy hell.

His words.

They possess me.

They command me.

They give me all the confidence I need to grip him in my hand, placing him at my entrance, and slowly lower myself down.

"Oh fuck. This feeling never gets old, Shay. You're so damn tight."

"Maybe it's because you're so big." I lean forward and kiss him.

"If you keep complimenting my dick like that, I'm going to come a lot faster than you want me to."

I seat myself fully on him and swirl my hips. "That's my goal."

This time when I lean forward to kiss him, I hover for a brief moment to whisper, "I want you to come so hard, you see stars."

Then I sit up, push my hands to his chest to lift my body just so before lowering again. I repeat over and over, up and down, his curses of pleasure like a song to my ears as I do exactly as he told me to and take what I want. When I feel the build begin, my nipples harden as if they're a beacon to him.

"Fuck me, Shay. Faster."

I close my eyes and do just that, but then he slaps my ass as I ride him and my eyes spring open.

"I want to see your eyes when you come. Don't you dare close them."

"I won't."

Then he sits up as I grind faster. His hand dips between us, and the finger that brushes against my clit makes me shatter all around him.

"Luca!" I scream and keep my pace until the sparks fade. I'm barely able to collect myself when Luca flips us, slams into me once, then twice, before pulling out and growling his orgasm as he comes all over my stomach.

The room is filled with our labored breaths as we try to calm down.

Resting back on his heels, my legs still open for his viewing, Luca slowly moves his gaze up to mine.

He grins. I'm pretty sure I blush. And then we both laugh.

"I love sex with you," he admits as he gets off the bed, strutting into the bathroom and returning with a warm towel. He kneels next to me and cleans my belly.

Then he tosses the towel into the laundry basket and crawls back into bed with me.

"I'm pretty fond of it myself," I say then kiss him.

We let it linger, his tongue slipping in to dance with mine before we're interrupted by the sound of my cell phone ringing on the nightstand.

He groans his disapproval.

"Let's just ignore the world today."

"I wish we could," I agree with him and suck in a breath. It's my brother's name on my screen.

"It's Leo."

I turn to look at Luca as he sits up on the bed, pulling the sheet to cover the bottom half of his body. I stare at his bare chest for a moment, knowing how firm it feels under my fingertips but still fighting the urge to reach out for him as if it's the first time.

"You better answer it. He'll be suspicious if you don't."

I nod and get up from the bed.

"Put clothes on first. If you walk around my house naked, our cover will be blown a lot sooner than you want it to be."

I grab his shirt from last night off the floor and slide it on.

"That doesn't exactly help."

I roll my eyes and answer the phone as I walk out to the living room.

"Hey, Leo," I say and sit on the sofa.

"Shay. What are you doing?"

He sounds upset.

"What do you mean what am I doing?"

"I mean, I called you three times and I tried The Marina, Carl said you weren't there yet."

He called three times? Shit.

"You did?"

"Yes. Are you okay? I was about to call Grace to see if something happened to you."

"I'm fine."

"Really? Because I know with Mom and Dad here this summer that leaves you all alone at The Marina and—"

"And I'm a grown woman who can be alone. Besides, I'm not alone."

"You're not? Who are you with?"

Oh, poor choice of words. I recover quickly.

"I mean, I have Grace and Brooke and the other girls here."

The line is silent for a second.

"You swear you're okay?"

"Yes. Please stop worrying."

"Okay, but it still feels like something is off. You never go to work this late."

"I …"

He's right, I don't.

"I just thought I'd take a slow morning. You and Mom and Dad are always saying I work too hard, so I listened."

"Okay." He blows out a breath. "How's The Marina coming along?"

"Good. Really good."

Luca appears in nothing but a pair of boxers, and my body moves toward him, my hands reaching out as if I'm an addict and need more of him.

"I'll call you later," I say quickly and hang up the phone.

I follow Luca into the kitchen and hop onto the counter next to where he's standing.

His gaze sweeps to mine, and he grins right before he picks me up, hauling me over his shoulder and walking right back to his room.

My laughter is the last thing we hear before he drops me to the bed, lifts his shirt so just my lower half is showing, and yanks me to the edge, hitting his knees.

I don't think I just like Luca anymore. I'm falling for him.

Which means … we need to have a plan.

And with the end of the summer quickly approaching, we need it soon.

But then he licks me right up the center, and all my worries vanish.

For now.

CHAPTER TWENTY

LUCA

I didn't warn my family that I was going to be bringing Shay to Sunday morning breakfast this week. I didn't need to warn them—they are all going to welcome her with open arms.

This does, however, mean there's a slight chance I'm going to have to explain what actually happened all those years ago with her brother. My family doesn't know how her family treated me and why we're no longer friends. They just know there was a falling out and I never wanted to talk about it.

Crazy thing is, after all these years and especially the past few weeks, I wouldn't trade any of it if it meant I'd end up in the place where I am now.

"You're sure that your family is going to be okay with this?"

Shay laces her fingers with mine and grips tighter.

"I'm sure."

"But, I mean, my family treated you so poorly. I was one of them. They have to know, right?"

"They know small pieces here and there, but mostly they just know that your brother and I had a falling out."

"So they don't know how my family treated you?"

I shake my head. "It's going to be fine. Now had I told them what happened all those years ago when it actually happened, yeah, they probably wouldn't be too impressed with you or anyone in your family. But it's been years, and according to Sadie, everyone has seen a difference in me in just the past three weeks. The moment I walk through the door with my hand in yours, they're going to know, if they don't already, that all those changes are because of you."

She groans, but she's smiling as she does it, so I know she likes what I just said.

"You are just so cheesy sometimes. I can't believe I never saw this before."

"Just because it's the truth doesn't mean it's cheesy."

"And there you go again, being extra cheesy."

"If it earns me the smile that's on your face right now, I'll be as cheesy as you want me to be."

She reaches across the truck, shoves my arm, then laughs.

"Stop it. Seriously, and don't flirt with me in front of your family. I don't need them to see how easily you win me over with your silliness. While we're at it, we may as well add that you shouldn't touch me either."

I let out a slight chuckle at her request. Not flirting with Shay sounds wrong. I only know one way to be around her, and I'm not going to change it just because there are other people around, especially not my family. Her family I'll make an exception for, until she is ready to tell them.

That's a whole other conversation the two of us need to have. We're both aware of how this summer is going to end, but I want us both to be on the same page when that time comes.

Her family is not going to be happy about our relationship, but I'll do anything she wants to keep it.

I pull my truck up in front of my sister's house, which used to be my dad's, then rush around the front of the hood to open the door for Shay. She rolls her eyes, which only makes me kiss her right there on the street for everyone in the town to see.

She kisses me back for a brief moment, but then she shoves my chest.

"Luca Asher, anybody could see us right now."

"If you think people in this town haven't caught on to the two of us at this point, you might not be made for small-town life."

"People aren't talking about us. Not like that."

I grab her hand and lead her up the sidewalk to the door. "They might not be talking about us, but they sure do know something's going on that we're not telling people about."

She looks up and down the street quickly.

"And how would they know that?"

"Well, I hate to break it to you, but The Marina is swiftly turning into a brand-new place and everyone is noticing."

Her lips fight a smile. She's probably thinking about how we ran into Mrs. W. that night and how not a single person since has mentioned us working together.

People, in fact, do know and aren't saying anything.

The respect small towns have for their own is one of a kind.

"I like knowing that people are talking about that place."

I nod.

"Me too."

I open the front door without knocking, pulling Shay inside with me.

It's not until I'm closing the door that it occurs to me that maybe I should have knocked. This is Ruby's house now. Walking into your sister's house is not the same as walking into your parents' place.

As if she knew I was talking about her, Ruby walks out from the kitchen.

The smile she wears as soon as she sees me and Shay is one I haven't seen in a really long time.

"You came," my sister says as she rushes to hug Shay. "I was hoping you would."

"It was getting hard to tell Luca no. He's asked me every week for a few of them now."

"I know. He would complain each Sunday that you didn't come."

Shay turns to me, her brows shooting up to her hairline.

"You've been talking about me to your family this whole time?"

I hold my hands up in surrender.

"They figured it out on their own, and once I knew they all knew, I swore them to secrecy."

"He really did," Ruby says. "Come on. Everyone is out back."

We follow her through the kitchen. It's a warm summer morning, so breakfast outside is refreshing.

Two kids whiz by as soon as we open the door.

"Max, Susie, go wash your hands," Ruby says. "It's almost time to eat."

"And don't say you don't need to. I saw you both digging for worms in the garden," Declan adds.

Ruby lets out a huff and walks back into the kitchen.

"I didn't know you were coming," I say to Declan and shake his hand.

"Yeah, neither did Ruby," he says, then looks at Hudson.

"What?" my oldest brother asks. "I truly didn't think she would care. Max and Susie are becoming little best friends. It made sense in my mind. I didn't know she couldn't stand him. Like really, *really* can't stand him."

"I told you that the other day," Declan adds.

"I thought you were being dramatic."

Declan stares at Hudson as if he has no idea how to reply to that. I get the sense that Declan isn't a dramatic man.

"Well, we are happy to have you," I say and take a seat at the table with Sadie and my dad, pulling out the chair next to me for Shay.

"Shay, hun, it's so good to see you again," my dad says. "I've missed having the Parker family around."

Guilt hits me instantly, and I know without looking at Shay that it's going to hit her, too.

I reach for her hand and hold it tight.

"I've missed you, too, Mr. Asher," Shay says at the same time.

"Does this mean that when your folks are back, we can all get together like the old days?"

Shay and I share a look.

A conversation I've been avoiding for years is finally here.

"Not exactly. Shay is the only Parker who still doesn't despise me."

"Is this the moment we all get to find out why?" Miles

says, stepping out from the sliding door with Quinn's hand in his.

"Don't jinx it," Hudson scolds him.

"My family accused Luca of stealing money from The Marina, and when he denied it, they accused him of lying too."

"Luca would never steal from The Marina," my dad says quickly.

"I know." Shay says, looking embarrassed. "I should have known that back then."

"So it was all a miscommunication. We could have fixed that."

Now it's my turn to be embarrassed.

"Well …"

"Did you do it?" Hudson asks, completely shocked.

"No, but I did sort of sleep with Leo's girlfriend at the time and made things worse."

"Who?" Hudson, Miles, and Shay all ask eagerly at the same time.

My dad adds a quiet "Good heavens."

Declan chuckles. "This is an exciting breakfast."

I shake my head.

"Her name was Indy."

The moment her name is off my lips, Shay breaks out into laughter.

"Leo broke up with Indy before someone stole the money, so I don't think he'd have been upset about that."

"What?"

I turn my focus to Shay. Her brother outright told me that because I slept with her, any chance we had of fixing things was gone. If he wasn't even dating her, why would he have been so dead set on us not being friends anymore? Outside of the money going missing, that is.

"Yeah, she was bad news. He made a lot of bad choices while he was dating her, and my parents said *no more*."

Shay picks a cut up strawberry and pops it into her mouth.

I'm so lost. So what else happened that summer?

I don't think I'm going to get any answers today. This is a lot to pack in. I spent the last decade and more thinking my choice was what sealed all this, but there had to be something else. What could it have been?

"So what do your parents think of the two of you together," my dad asks, "if they think my son is a thief."

Shay cringes. "They don't know about us … yet."

The fact that she added on the *yet* is the only reason I'm not spiraling out over why we are still a secret to most of the town.

She plans to tell them the truth.

That moment is going to be one of the best of my life, I can feel it.

"So if you didn't steal the money, who did?" Quinn asks.

"We don't know," Shay answers.

As if I can sense him looking at me, I meet Miles's gaze. He mouths *Leo* to me, and suddenly all the dots connect.

If Leo was making bad choices, stealing money could have been one of them.

The thing that boggles me is why, after all these years, if it was him, hasn't he come clean?

"Speaking of The Marina, when can we see it?" Ruby asks. She brings the last tray of food to the table and takes a seat. The kids dig in first, stealing most of Sadie's famous quiche.

"Soon." The pride that beams off my girl is a sight to see.

There is no way her parents can come back, see that place, and decide to sell it to someone else.

As soon as breakfast is over, Shay and I get back in my truck.

I have a surprise for her for the rest of our day.

"Where are we going?" she asks as I turn onto the highway that leads out of town instead of toward The Marina.

I grab her hand, bring it to my lips, and kiss the back of it.

"We are going to Wind Valley."

"For what?"

"So that I can take you on a proper date where I can kiss you as much as I want and hold your hand as much as I want."

"There you go again," she says with a massive smile on her lips.

"What?"

"Being cheesy." I shrug as she leans over the center to kiss my cheek. "But I really like cheesy."

"Good, because once you've been on a date with me, there is no going back."

"I'm pretty sure there's no going back as it is. You don't need to court me at this point."

Her words hit me in the chest.

They're exactly what I needed to hear.

There's no going back.

CHAPTER TWENTY-ONE

SHAY

Watching Luca move around The Marina as if he belongs here just as much as I do never gets old.

Yesterday all the new tables and chairs showed up for the dining room, and Luca has been moving them in and the old ones out all day.

I finally caved after that day with his family and let him work anytime he wants. The town obviously knows—we may as well use it to our advantage and get things done.

I'll admit, working during the day is much more effective. It also gives me more time with Luca.

This summer started stressful, but it's turning out to be so much better than I could have ever hoped. The stress is still there since I don't know the outcome of The Marina yet, but having Luca here helps.

Adding final touches in the dining room makes everything finally feel worth it, even if we still have the cabins to finish.

"To be honest, I wasn't sure this moment would ever get here."

Luca looks up from where he's screwing in legs to one of the tables.

"What do you mean? This place looks great."

"I know it does, but last summer, I wasn't so convinced."

I move my paint bucket down an inch as I keep painting the walls where we added batten boards.

His screwdriver hits the floor with a plunk, and he grins, sauntering toward me.

"No. Stop. We need to finish."

My brother and parents will be here next week, and I want the main building and at least three cabins to be officially done. Not nearly done, but *done*, down to the last detail. Part of me thinks that if Luca and I didn't end up fooling around every night the past few weeks, I'd be there already.

I'm not complaining, per se. I'd rather be behind schedule because I'm stupid happy when I'm with him than for the reasons before I hired him.

Still, I need this done. If it's finished when they all get back to the States, then maybe they will take the news of me dating Luca better and wait until I can afford to buy The Marina.

I haven't decided how I'm going to tell them. I just know I need to tell them sooner rather than later, and somehow, I need to convince them that Luca didn't steal from them all those years ago. It would be a lot easier to do if I knew who actually did it though.

My time to make a plan is running out.

Which is why …

"Stop," I say and hold out my hand. "If you come any closer, we won't finish this room tonight, and then I'll have to get started early tomorrow."

Luca chuckles, but he stops.

He crosses his arms.

"How about we take a break, work late—with another break—and then I sleep over and we both get started early tomorrow?"

It's a valid plan. One that does include a lot of working, but if he spends the night, there will be little sleeping and that affects the way we—

"You're thinking way too hard over this." He moves closer.

"I just want it to be ready now."

The grin he sports as he takes the last few steps to reach me melts my heart. It's the smile he reserves just for me. I call it his *I'm proud of you* smile. The one he gives me when he wants to compliment me, but he doesn't know the words to use.

"This place is ready, Shay. Trust me. No one even notices the small details you do. All they see now is the life you brought back to this place."

He brushes the wisps of hair that have fallen into my face behind my ear.

"I've never felt more at home than I do standing right here, right now, with you."

Home. That's the exact vibe I want this place to give people.

A Hozier song comes through the speaker, and Luca plucks the paintbrush from my hand, sets it down, then pulls me into the middle of the room.

"Luca, we can't just dance in the middle of the room. People will see us."

"Well," he says and leans in to whisper in my ear, "It's a

good thing most of this town already knows that I belong to you, isn't it?"

It's so cliché, but his words make my heart swell. My eyes sting with unshed tears as I think about how, even after all we've been doing this summer, I could have let this man slip by me.

I reach up, my hand cupping his face as I press my lips to his.

I intend for it to be a sweet, gentle kiss, but as soon as I push to my toes, my body brushes his. He wraps his arms around my waist to hold me tighter and deepen the kiss. Then he spins me, bumps me into a table, and picks me up to sit on it. My legs open for him to stand between them.

"Ouch!" I say and pull back, reaching into his pocket to pull out his keys. I drop them onto the table then pull him back to me as if I'm starved. "Don't lose them. We might need them in a few minutes to get out of here."

He lets out a growl and kisses me as if I were his air. His hands are cupping my face, and mine are gripping his shirt, pulling it from where it was tucked into his jeans.

I know someone could see us, but I don't care right now.

Right now, the only thing that matters is—

"Oh, fuck."

My heart races at the unfamiliar voice, and I peek around Luca to see who it belongs to. We look at the door at the same time, both freezing when we set eyes on the man who fills the doorway.

My brother.

CHAPTER TWENTY-TWO

LUCA

Leo Parker's hands are clenched at his sides, and his jaw is tight. He looks as if he's seconds away from punching me in the face.

The smart thing to do right now would be to back away from his sister. If anything, moving to stand anywhere that isn't between her legs seems best, but I don't even flinch.

Neither does Shay.

Well, she doesn't for all but thirty seconds anyway.

She pushes me back with her feet, and I go because if that's what she wants, I'll give it to her. This moment right here isn't just about me.

In fact, it's a topic we've both been avoiding.

I know we have our own opinions on how this should play out and we both assumed we had more time, but I'm wishing that we'd had discussed it right about now.

"Leo." Shay stands, adjusting her shorts into place. She pulls her shirt down as if she'd been flashing him, which she wasn't, and then she takes a tentative step toward her brother. "What are you doing here?"

"What am I doing?" He huffs. "What are you doing, Shay?"

"Hey," I snap, not pausing long enough to think of how this might play out before I go on. "Don't talk to her with that tone."

"She's my sister. I'll talk to her however I want, Asher."

I shake my head.

"Sister or not, calm your tone."

Leo takes a step toward me, but Shay steps between us before he can reach me.

"Stop."

"What's he doing here, Shay?" Leo asks, and I'll be damned, he corrected his tone.

I chuckle.

Shay hesitates, looking at me briefly before addressing her brother. Quietly, she says, "I hired him to help me finish The Marina."

"You're joking, right?"

"Does it look like I'm joking, Leo?" she yells and holds her arms out. "I'm the only one in this family who cares about this place, and it needed to be done, so I did it. You do not get to stand here and tell me how to do anything when I'm the only one putting in the time."

You tell him, baby!

"You know how Mom and Dad will feel about this."

Shay groans, and I swear, for a fleeting moment, he looks at me with guilt in his eyes.

Shay drops into a chair, her shoulders drooping and her

head down, her face in her hands. I step toward her, but Leo shoves me back.

"Don't."

"Don't what? Comfort her when you're being a dick?"

"Luca, I swear to god, if you—"

"Enough!" Shay yells and then stands. "I'm not doing this right now. I have better things to do than listen to you two fight."

Leo glares at me as if this is my fault, and sure, yeah, from Shay's outburst, it's clear I partially am to blame, but it's not just on me.

However, when Shay looks up at me through those dark lashes and her eyes plead with me to help her, I don't have to think twice.

"I'll give you two some space," I say, hating every single word, but I know that the sooner she gets things cleared with her brother and her family, the sooner she can relax and get back to focusing on The Marina.

I don't want her spending one more minute worried over this.

"Thank you," she whispers.

I nod, then kiss the top of her head as I leave. "Call me when you're done."

"Okay."

I rub her back for a split second.

"Let her talk before you freak out, okay?" I tell Leo.

Leo rolls his eyes..

On my way out, I pass the bar and wave to Carl and Matt. Since this place has picked up, they've both been working full-time, and then I walk out the main door.

The timing of her brother coming back is unfortunate. It

would have been great if Shay was able to break the news of our relationship before he saw it in action, but life never works out that way.

Heck, despite the tension just now, perhaps this could mend things. Our families used to be close. Maybe there's a chance they still could be.

God, I hope they give her a chance to talk.

I walk up to my truck and reach into my pocket to unlock the door.

I don't feel my keys.

Shit. I left them in the room with Shay and her brother.

I turn, jogging back to the dining room to get in and out so they can have their privacy.

I've got one foot through the door when I freeze.

"So it's nothing?"

"No. It's not serious. I'm not sure about Luca, but it's just fun for me, and I—"

Shay's words halt when she sees me in the doorway.

Now, I know the situation, all right? I know that she's probably stressed and unsure of how to answer, but let me be clear, this is not just fun for me. It's never been just fun for me. I was all in, and until this moment, I thought Shay was too.

Maybe you are only good enough as a secret.

No one says anything. I glance from Shay to her brother and then back to Shay.

I wait for her to say something, but she doesn't.

All she does is stand slowly.

"I, uh," I clear my throat. "I forgot my keys."

I move for the table and grab them, turning for the door

without another word. Shay's lack of response right now is all I need to know.

I'm the guy women fool around with in secret.

Fuck, that sucks.

"Luca, wait," Shay calls out to me as I exit.

I don't stop.

"Luca, please wait."

Against my better judgment, I pause and turn slowly.

"Did you mean that?" I ask.

"I just need time to figure things out."

"Figure things out," I repeat. "About us?"

"No, no, I just—"

"Because from what I just heard, there is no us."

"Luca, I just … I need … I …"

I nod slowly.

Wow.

Wow.

Fuck. This is unbelievable.

"I'm a fool," I say and then walk away.

"No. You're not. Luca, wait."

She rushes after me, but I'm not stopping this time.

I'm not asking for a lot. Just the truth, and right now, I don't think Shay even knows what it is.

I want someone I can trust, and right now that person is not the woman following me.

"Luca, please."

I open my door and get in, but the window is down, so I can still hear her pleas.

"Let me call you later. Let me figure this out. Let me … no, don't back away. Please, don't go. Wait. Just wait until I can fix this. Don't go. Please."

It's too late.

She was quick to pretend like what we had wasn't real. When the time came that I needed her to pick me, pick us, she didn't.

I'm not going through this again.

I won't.

Even if it means losing the one and only woman I've ever fallen in love with.

CHAPTER TWENTY-THREE

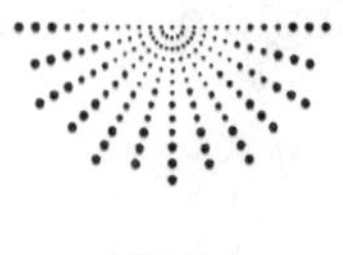

SHAY

The tears are uncontrollable as I race back into The Marina.

"Shay, what the fuck has been going on here this summer?"

"No!" I point to the door. "You don't get to walk in here and ask questions. Not right now."

"You can't trust him," Leo argues quickly. "He—"

"He said he didn't do it, and I believe him,, and I … I …"

I glance back at the door, wiping the tears from my cheeks.

"I have to go find him."

"I thought you said it was just fun for you."

"I lied, okay?"

"Jesus, Shay, why?"

"Because! I knew what might happen if Mom and Dad found out that I hired him. They'll take this family business away from me without asking for the full story, just like you didn't moments ago. So I lied, and now I have to fix this."

I grab my purse from behind the bar and rush out of The

Marina. I know my brother is behind me, but I don't care. He can watch if he wants. I made a poor choice for a split second, and everything ignited from there.

"I'm heading out," I tell Carl and rush out the door.

I break into a jog as I head into town.

The first place I stop is Hudson's Bar. It hasn't been long since Luca left our job site, and there are only a few places he would go.

I swing the door open with more force than normal, causing everyone to look at me. I can't imagine what they see. A woman with mascara running down her face, all sweaty from her run.

"Have you seen Luca?" I ask Hudson the moment I see him behind the bar.

"Shay, wait," I hear my brother behind me. I glance back to see him getting out of his truck.

I ignore him and look at Hudson again.

"Luca. Is he here?" I ask with more desperation.

Hudson's eyes widen as he glances between me and my brother.

With his hands on his hips, he drops his chin to his chest and shakes his head.

"He's not here."

"Do you know where he might be?" I ask, moving closer.

Hudson looks up, and I can see the worry in his eyes.

"No, but I'll help you look for him."

"Thank you. Please have him call me when you find him."

Hudson nods and gives me a smile filled with sympathy. "I'll tell him."

"Shay." My brother grabs my arm gently. "We need to talk."

"I don't want to talk to you," I say sharply and then rush out the door.

The only person I want to talk to is Luca.

I spend the next hour checking his shop, his house, the bar again, Brooke's bakery, and I even go by his dad's and Ruby's, but he isn't there. I call him no less than a dozen times, filling his voice mailbox to capacity.

But none of it works. He doesn't answer, he doesn't reply to my texts, and he doesn't call me back.

Defeated, I start my walk home. I've made it as clear as I can that I'm sorry and that what I did was wrong. Now I need to give him time to decide what he wants to do next.

I hope it's to come find me.

By the time I make it back to my house, my parents are sitting out on my patio, waiting for me.

I don't think it's possible for me to cry more today than I already have today.

Which is probably a good thing, because as soon as I hit my front door, I know my parents are going to tell me how disappointed they are in me and no matter how hard I worked this summer, they still plan to sell The Marina.

It just seems like such a load of crap to me that their grown daughter is asking them to wait and sell her The Marina, and they won't do it. If anyone gets to be mad right now, it should be me.

"Shay, honey, how is your day going?"

My mom's voice is calm, but the concern laced in each word is a dead giveaway that she's already talked to Leo.

"That's the opening question you have for me?"

My mother grins softly, her green eyes shining as she smiles.

"What else am I supposed to say? I can already see on your face that today has not been good to you."

"Not to mention your brother has already called and given us a little rundown of how your summer's been going," my father adds with the smallest smirk.

It's not the reaction I'm expecting.

"I know exactly what you're going to say."

"Do you?" my mother asks.

"Yes. You're going to tell me that I've done the absolute unthinkable to this family and betrayed everyone by hiring Luca. You're going to tell me, once again, that you're not going to sell me The Marina because of the choices I made while you were gone. Well, I don't need you to tell me something I already know."

My father crosses his arms and gets that scowl in his eyes that he used to give Leo and me as kids when we did something we weren't supposed to do.

"You might be a grown woman, but you could cool the tone when you're talking to your mother."

I take a deep breath. He's right. I'm mad, and speaking this way isn't going to change it.

"All right then, tell me what you came here to say." I move past my parents to sit on the swinging chair. They both study me as I sit, my arms crossed, ready to argue with whatever they want to say to me. Mom's eyes gloss over while Dad's scream with concern.

I knew it.

I don't know why they think it's important that they have to actually say the words to me. I just said them.

"We already spoke with a realtor prior to us finding out that you hired Luca to help you with the remodel, so I just need you to know that *your* choices had nothing to do with *our* choice."

Turns out, I do have more tears for the day.

My mother moves quickly to join me on the swing. She grabs my hand then she hooks me.

"We want you to know that this has nothing to do with our trust in you and the way you could run The Marina. It's a lot to take in—it took a lot away from us, caused a lot of fights, and stole family trips we could have taken. We don't want the same thing for you."

"But isn't that for me to decide? Don't I get to be the one who decides my future? That place holds so many memories for me. I want to make more."

My father nods slowly. "Honey, we hear you, but we've already made up our minds, and the money from the sale will help us fulfill our retirement plans."

I hear them, and I understand that they earned the right to do what they want for retirement. I just … this is my dream, and I can't accept that no matter how much love and heart and time I gave it, it's not going to come true.

"Please, please just wait until I can figure something out."

My mom starts to cry as she hugs me.

"I wish we could, but it's time for someone else to love that place."

They let me cry for a good ten minutes, and when I'm done, my mother asks, "Do you want to tell us what's going on with Luca?"

I glance between them. Neither of them look upset, which, again, is not what I expected.

"I … I think I'm in love with him," I admit, getting right to the point.

"Think or know?" my dad asks.

"Know."

"So what's the problem?"

"I hurt him. I lied to Leo about our relationship, thinking you'd all be disappointed in me and sell The Marina because of it, but I guess it didn't matter, because you're selling it anyway. Now I've lost The Marina and Luca."

My head drops back as the realization hits me.

My heart feels like it's being squeezed, and I break into tears again.

"You go ahead and cry, honey, but my advice is that when you're done, you start making a plan to make it up to him. If he loves you even an ounce of how much you love him, you won't be apart for very long."

"But you hate him."

My mom gasps.

"We do not."

"You do, too. You told me not to hire him."

Dad winces. "And we were wrong."

"So wrong. He didn't steal that money, and we treated him horribly."

"I know," Dad says and I jerk back.

"You knew?"

He nods. "As of about an hour ago when your brother came to find us."

"But, how, what … and you just believe him now? And not Luca back then."

"Yes."

"Why?"

"Because Leo told us the truth. It was him who stole the money and not Luca."

My eyes go so wide I swear they might fall out, but like I have all afternoon, that emotion quickly reverts back to crying.

No wonder Luca is so upset.

My family has been betraying him for more than a decade.

And after today, I'm no different.

CHAPTER TWENTY-FOUR

LUCA

For the last two days, I've done nothing but work. I'm the first one at the shop the next morning. I've already got the trucks loaded and ready before anyone else shows up. Benson walks in and whistles.

"Early morning?" he asks.

"Yep."

"Any particular reason?"

"Nope."

He nods slowly.

"Well, thanks for getting things ready. Are you going to be working with us today or just stopping in?"

I think about his question.

The busier I am, the less time I have to think about Shay.

About how I fell so fucking in love with a woman who can't even tell her family about me. Can't, won't, it doesn't matter.

Being with someone and finding out that they don't want to claim you hurts like hell.

My chest feels tight thinking about it; my throat goes dry and my eyes burn when I think about her.

Everyone is always so worried about the girl getting her heart broken—well, news flash, a man's heart can break just as easily. Shay took mine and smashed it with a sledgehammer.

"I'm working with you," I say to Benson, who is still waiting for an answer.

"Cool. That means we might finish some projects today."

I chuckle, knowing that an extra pair of hands on any job means more work gets done, but too bad for them that my head and heart are distracted. I'll be there in body, but my mind will be elsewhere.

Once everyone shows up and takes a company truck to start the day, I get in my own vehicle and head out for the first job site.

I let out a breath.

For the day only, because working tonight at The Marina is not an option. Not anymore.

I reach the first site of the day, put my truck in park, then my phone beeps with a text.

I pull it out of my pocket as if it zapped me.

MILES

Are you working today?

LUCA

I work every day.

MILES

I know. I'm just checking in.

HUDSON

What he really wants to ask is, how are you today?

LUCA

I'm fine.

MILES

Be serious.

LUCA

I am serious.

MILES

And that right there is the problem. You don't do serious.

Miles has added Ruby to the chat.

HUDSON

He's right. I miss goofy Luca.

LUCA

I'm just busy.

MILES

Being sad.

RUBY

Lighten up on him, you two! His heart is hurting.

MILES

What do you know?

HUDSON

He told you?

I groan and slide my phone back into my pocket. Twice a day now, they check in on how I'm doing. I haven't shared many details, but they know it has to do with Shay. If Ruby knows, it's because she's talked to Shay.

Something I haven't done because I still have no idea what I'd say that's different from what I said before.

Heartbreak is a weird thing.

I'm still living and all that, but I feel like a part of me died. A part that was filled with happiness and plans for the future.

I don't fucking know.

I just know that I'm going through the motions, but I feel like a part of me is missing.

And I want it back, but I don't know if I could go through this again.

On a groan, I get out of the truck. I wish I knew which direction my personal life is going.

But until I figure things out, work is all I need.

———

"COULD YOU JUST TALK OR SOMETHING?" Hudson says, arms folded as he glares at me from the other side of the bar top.

"I'm eating lunch. What more do you want from me?"

"Well, more than what you're giving. Seriously, you're giving me some 'I'm about to punch you in the face' vibes."

I let out a huff laugh and stab my fork into my salad. "Well, I'm about to if you don't stop telling me to act differently."

He steps closer and leans down in front of me.

"Did I tell you that Shay came in looking for you the other day?"

I refuse to look at him.

I figured he knew something was up when he found me sitting in his apartment the other day. I didn't really know where to go, but I knew I'd be alone there, with Hudson and Sadie both working. He didn't say a word, just asked if I wanted dinner and went on with his day.

It seems though, he was waiting to say more.

"She was in a panic and wanted to know where you were. She had tears running down her face, and she looked—"

"I don't care," I cut him off.

His eyes go wide.

"Shay and I aren't a thing anymore."

"Yeah, I gathered that. I still think we should—"

"I don't want to talk about it."

"Luca, man, come on. You're clearly upset over it and—"

"I said I don't want to talk about it." My voice is firm enough that Hudson flinches and steps back.

"Sure. But take it from someone who's been in your place before, the—"

"Have you really? Have you been in love with a woman who was too scared of what her family would think of the two of you, so she just … forget it."

I stand, toss some money on the bar, and start to walk out.

Hudson grabs my shirt.

"I've been in a place where I thought the love of my life just walked out the fucking door and wasn't coming back. I've been in a place where I thought that me—all of me and who I am—wasn't going to be enough for her. That's where I've been."

He lets go of my shirt and shoves me back.

"Now, when you decide you're done being a dick and finished with your pity party, we can fix this together."

His words cool my anger, but they don't change the outcome.

"There is no fixing it, Hudson. It was clear that she had doubts about us. She lied so easily and that … you just can't fix that."

I don't wait for him to say more.

I just walk out the door and move on with my day.

CHAPTER TWENTY-FIVE

LUCA

Most of the guys are at my house after I get off work.

Hudson decided that tonight was a fucking swell time for boys' night.

He was wrong.

So, so wrong.

I wasn't included in the text, or I would have voiced that opinion.

Yep, it's been a whole five hours since I was sitting in his bar eating lunch. He said he'd give me space to stop being a dick, but apparently, that meant dinner time was my cutoff.

"Dude, you're being a real downer, and today is a good day. It's been a good couple of weeks, actually."

I glare at Miles.

The ending to his summer versus mine are not the same.

"What's going on? For real this time," he asks and sits up, attempting to look innocent. As if he and Hudson never talk.

I don't say anything.

Declan walks through the door with a six-pack and some chips.

"I've got one hour and then I need to walk back to my house," he says, quickly setting his things down and twisting the top off a beer. "Your sister is watching Susie and made it very clear I'm on a time limit."

Dutton walks in next. He's got his head down, looking at his phone. It reminds me of Grace in a way. That family is all business. This is probably the most social Dutton gets.

Sucks for him that I'm not in the mood.

I'm going to ruin everyone's night.

I'll blame it on Hudson.

"Good. Everyone is here," Hudson says as if he's a judge waiting for all parties to arrive before we begin the night. "Shay and Luca broke up, I think."

"Seriously?" I groan. "An announcement?"

"Yes. The sooner we talk it out and make a plan, the sooner you can get the girl back. I wish someone had helped me sooner. Every day without Sadie was hell. I never wish that pain on anyone."

"Yeah, well"—I grab a beer—"Shay and I are not you and Sadie."

"Principles still apply," he says.

Why doesn't anyone get it? I wasn't enough for her. She was fine tossing out everything we shared together like the trash in the back room just so her brother wouldn't be upset with her.

Who does that?

I'm the guy you keep as a secret. I'm never the real thing.

It's a shitty fucking feeling that I don't know how to

explain to anyone, and I don't want to. I don't want to talk about it.

"Just go talk to her," Miles grumbles after I refuse to stop scowling.

"No."

"Run it by us what happened," Linc says.

"It's not worth it."

"Just tell us," Dutton says. He's set his phone down and is fully invested in this conversation. I glance around at all of them. All eyes are on me.

"If I tell you, can we drop it?"

They nod.

I give them a quick recap of what happened after Leo showed up at The Marina.

"She messed up, okay?" Miles speaks first. "She panicked and said it meant nothing, but you know it does."

"Well then, that's what she should have said. Not … what actually came out." I blow out a breath, feeling my heart strain all over again. "The point is, if at one point she was embarrassed or whatever, then she could feel that way again."

"Whatever the point is, Luca, you can't fix it unless you two talk to each other."

"And say what? Hey, just curious, are you sure you weren't lying, and if you were, why did you? And also, can you not do that again so that we can be together?"

Dutton's head bounces side to side. "In a way, yeah. You're the most honest person I know. Tell it to her straight."

They make it sound so easy.

"I … it's not that easy, guys."

"Do you want to patch things up with Shay?" Miles asks to clarify.

"I … yes, of course. I just—fuck, why is this so hard?"

"Go talk to her. Whoever put this idea out there that the one who fucked up has to be the one to fix it was dumb. Relationships are a team effort. Tell her what you want and what you expect from her. If she doesn't want it, she can tell you."

"I don't know, that sounds awfully dominant," I mutter.

I smirk a little.

Shay does like it when I take control and boss her around, so maybe telling her exactly what I want is the right move. It doesn't need to be flashy, just the truth.

"Let's change the subject, please."

"I was thinking of signing us up as a basketball team," Linc says out of the complete fucking blue.

"Does anyone here actually play basketball?" Declan asks. "Outside of knowing the basics?"

We all shake our heads.

"All the more reason to do it." Linc's attention turns to his phone just as there's a knock at the door that makes us all pause.

We all glance around the room as if we need to double-check the count of people here. Hudson, Miles, Dutton, Declan, and Linc. Everyone is accounted for.

Maybe it's my dad.

I get up to answer the door and scowl as soon as I see the face on the other side.

Leo Parker.

From the corner of my eye, I see Hudson and Miles both stand.

"I'm not here to start anything," Leo says quickly. "Can I come in?"

This is the first time that he's ever come to me.

I step back and wave him in.

He slowly moves into the living room.

"Are you having a party?" he asks.

I open my mouth to say it's just a casual hangout, but Linc beats me to it.

"It's boys' night. Want a beer?"

Leo looks over his shoulder at me. His left brow raises, and I can read his expression, exactly the same way I could back in high school.

I let out a small laugh.

"Yep. Boys' night, but you don't get a beer."

"Fair enough."

"Why are you here?" I ask, not waiting for him to start this conversation.

"I'm here for Shay."

"Good," Miles says. "We were just making a plan for Luca to win her back."

"Miles. Fuck. Chill."

He laughs, holding his hands up. "Sorry. We were though."

I kind of miss when he was quiet and broody all the time.

Love does weird things to people.

"I want to help," Leo adds, shocking us all.

"What?"

He lets out a long sigh. "Look, you dating my sister isn't ideal, but I've never seen her like this, and over the summer— well, before you started working together—anytime I called, she talked about The Marina and nothing else. Her plans for it and how much progress she'd made. Which was great, because she loves that place, but it was her whole life. Then one day, I called and her voice was different. She sounded lighter, and if she wasn't telling me about something cool she'd done, she was rushing to get off the phone. I'm assuming to see you. Whatever. I could tell something changed. I didn't know what it was, but I knew it was good. Imagine my shock when I caught you with her."

I rub the back of my neck.

"Surprise," I say, and a couple of the guys behind me laugh awkwardly.

Leo grins for a split second. "I know it wasn't you who stole from The Marina."

"What?" I ask at the same time as Hudson and Miles.

"Yeah, I … it was me."

Holy shit.

"You stole the money?"

He nods.

"And you let your family think it was me."

He nods.

"All this time?"

He nods again. "Well, until the day I caught you and Shay."

I have no words. I just stare at him.

"I know. It's … I was too embarrassed back then, and time went on and my pride got the best of me. Not to mention, you slept with my girlfriend."

"Ex," Hudson and Miles both say.

I glare at them and then return my focus to Leo.

"That's what Shay told us."

"She was right. I stole the money just to impress that girlfriend, and when she told me to do it again, I dumped her."

I nod and then sit.

"I can't believe it was you. That was a dick move to let me fall for it."

"Yeah, it was. I'm sorry."

He sits next to me, and I don't need to think twice about my response.

"You're forgiven."

"Thanks, man. Now that that's out of the way, I need you to know something else."

"There's more?" Declan says with an eagerness I've never heard. I swear his eyes even light up.

Again, all the attention is on me.

It's weird, but at the same time, I feel oddly supported right now.

Is that why girls' nights started?

"What else is there?"

He lets out an even bigger sigh than before he told me that he was the thief.

"My parents are putting The Marina on the market next week."

I stand quickly and glare at him.

"You're joking?"

He shakes his head.

"But that place is like home to Shay and me, to all of us. Shay just spent the summer pouring her heart into that place. Do they already have a buyer?"

"Not yet, but the place looks really good, thanks to you and Shay. It'll sell quickly."

I scrub my hands over my face.

How is Shay taking this? Is she okay? I should have called her. Been there for her. Found a way to make it better or help her or … I don't know. She hurt me, but my heart still wants her to have everything she wants in life. Including The Marina.

"I'll buy it."

"What?"

"I'll buy it," I repeat.

"Luca, you can't just decide to buy it on a whim like this."

"I can and I will. Tell them to sell it to me. Better yet, I'm going to their house right now to ask them." I turn my attention to Linc. "Send me everything I need to know so I can make an offer in the morning as soon as I leave the bank."

"Luca, you already own a business," Leo says, as if I don't know this already.

"So, I'll own two."

The room falls silent, until Hudson leans forward.

"Since you're being all crazy right now, I … ugh, I have an idea."

I meet his eyes and watch as a grin takes over.

I know what he's going to say before he says it.

I'm in.

I just need to convince her parents first.

NOSTALGIA HITS me hard as I walk up the path to Mr. and Mrs. Parker's front door. It's been years since I've been here, yet every memory of running this exact sidewalk and bursting through the door without knocking hits me hard.

Like it was yesterday.

But today, my steps are focused and I knock, waiting for one of them to open the door.

I'm also praying they don't slam it in my face.

Thanks to Leo apologizing and coming clean less than an hour ago, I have a hunch they won't shut me out, but it's been a long time.

I'm not sure what I can expect right now.

This whole summer has been filled with surprises.

I hear the lock click on the other side, and slowly, the door opens. Mrs. Parker sighs and smiles.

"Luca Asher, this is a sight I was convinced I'd never see again."

"You and me both."

She steps back and waves me inside.

"I had a feeling you'd be coming by soon. I just wasn't expecting it today."

"Yeah, Leo hadn't even left my house before I grabbed my keys and headed this way. What I have to say can't wait."

She nods.

"Hun!" she calls out, and Mr. Parker appears from the hallway that leads to Leo and Shay's childhood rooms. His office is also back there. The same pictures from when we were kids line the walls and the same furniture we'd all pass out on after a long day in the sun still sit in the front living room.

No matter how long it's been, I still feel at home here.

"Luca," he says with surprise, his hands on his hips as he looks me over. "It's good to see you."

"It's good to see you both, too."

I fear an awkward silence is about to fill the air. There are so many things to say, yet none of us have any idea where to begin.

"Let's go to the dining room, and I'll get some lemonade," Mrs. Parker says. "I made cookies, too."

I chuckle. Some things never change.

Mrs. Parker works quickly, and within minutes, the three of us sit down.

"I just want to start by saying that I am so, so, *so* sorry that we didn't believe you, Luca," Mr. Parker starts the conversation.

Mrs. Parker sucks in a breath, and I look in time to catch her swiping away a tear.

"You don't need to apologize," I start and then look at Shay's mom again. "And you definitely don't need to cry. Leo's your kid. You should 100 percent believe him over me."

"But it's you," Mrs. Parker whispers. "We knew you just as well as we knew him."

I reach for her hand.

"It's okay."

"It's not, though."

Her response makes me grin.

"Now I know where Shay gets her stubbornness."

Mr. Parker laughs, and his wife finally nods.

"Which brings me to why I'm really here. I'm not here for apologies. I don't need them, but what I do need is for you to sell The Marina to me so that I can put it in Shay's and my name together."

"Luca," Mr. Parker says softly and starts to shake his head. "We don't want to put the burden of that place on Shay."

"It wouldn't be on Shay alone. It would be both her and I, and with all due respect, that place is not a burden. Not to me and definitely not to Shay."

He sighs. "It'll take up too much of her time—and yours —and we just don't want that for her."

"You two deserve to have freedom and not be tied down to a place that takes so much attention," Mrs. Parker chimes in.

"I think that's a choice for Shay and I to make. She's done so much to that place over the summer, and the way it's changed in just a matter of months is only the beginning of how amazing she can and will make it."

"Luca, this is very admirable of you, but we just can't," Mr. Parker says with finality.

His shoulders are drooping and she's frowning.

"Who do you plan to sell it to?" I ask.

"There is a gentleman from Wind Valley coming to look at it tomorrow."

I nod slowly, then do my best to look them both in the eye as I speak.

"If you sell it to him, I'll just go to him and convince him to sell it to me. I'll do it with whomever you choose to sell it to. They might make me pay twice or even triple your current selling price, but it'll be worth it to watch Shay's dreams come true, to be by her side when it happens. Because no matter how this works out, I will find a way to get that woman every bit of the life she wants and deserves, and once she forgives me for being an asshat these past few days, I'm going do everything in my power to show her that I've never loved anyone more than I love her. I'll spend day after day showing her that if she wants it, I want it—and we want that Marina."

I hold my chin high, so they know I'm not kidding around.

Mr. and Mrs. Parker share a look that it seems only they can understand.

When neither of them speak, I stand.

"You might not have believed me back then, but I need

you to believe me now. I will do whatever it takes to get Shay that marina, even if I have to sell my own company to do it."

I head for the door. I'm just about to turn the handle when Mr. Parker clears his throat.

"If anyone in our family can bring that place back to life, it's Shay. Despite all of this, I do want this for her, too. Get your offer to Linc by dinner tomorrow and you've got yourself a deal. If Shay is going on this journey, I can't imagine a better man to be at her side."

And then he hugs me.

I don't cry, but damn, knowing they trust me again after all these years, that they trust me when it comes to their daughter and her dreams … if a moment is going to count, it's this one.

CHAPTER TWENTY-SIX

SHAY

The dining room has a waitlist.

I stand back and look into the space, loving how the end result makes it feel so cozy.

I'd pulled an all-nighter the night Luca left to get it ready. I knew he wasn't coming back to help, and despite my family selling, I needed to see it in full swing again.

People are eating, laughing, and some are taking group pictures.

It's exactly what I wanted for this place.

It's what I worked hard for, and it's … not going to be mine.

I sigh and head down the hallway with its fresh paint and lined with pictures from my childhood: some of the events we held back then, some just of random ones my family or Luca's family took. A majority of them include my family and his, and that's okay. The history of this place really hit us the deepest.

And soon it'll go to another family.

I hope they have kids.

I hope they want to make memories the way I did, and I hope they don't change everything Luca and I just poured our hearts into.

I don't think I could come back if they gutted it.

I'm just about to turn into the office when Ruby calls my name.

"Hi." She beams and then hugs me. "How are you?"

I know she's asking out of pure friendliness, but the look in her eyes says she's not just asking about my day.

"I'm doing okay."

The truth is, I hurt. My heart, my head, every piece of me.

Luca still hasn't called or texted or anything.

I thought he would have reached out by now.

I want to apologize and tell him that it will never happen again.

I was scared, and what I did was wrong. I fully messed up.

It's been three days, and I'm starting to think that I'm not going to get the chance to tell him any of that.

"Are you really?"

I shrug and force a smile as my eyes start to burn with tears.

"It's all I can be right now."

"Oh, Shay." She pulls me in for another hug.

The tears are uncontrollable.

She nods toward my office, and I follow her in.

"I messed up so bad," I say, but I'm sobbing now, and I'm not sure she can understand me. "I spent the last two years giving this place my all, and I was scared that it was all about to be taken from me."

"I know." She rubs my back. "I know."

"And now I'm losing it anyway, and I lost Luca, too."

I drop my face into my hands and just let myself cry. I cried the night he left, but I've felt pretty numb since then.

It's a weird feeling when you realize that even though you gave it your heart and soul and manifested it as hard as you could, the dream you spent your whole life imagining is just … gone.

I know how dramatic that sounds, but I saw it. My life. Here. Forever. And then this summer happened, and I saw that life with Luca.

Fear makes people do stupid things and now I'm paying for it.

"Have you tried to call him again?"

I shake my head.

"I figure that after he ignored ten of my calls the first two days, he knows to call me when he's ready. If he's ever going to be ready."

With a big sigh, Ruby sits on the edge of the desk.

"He'll come around; I know he will. I just wish I could tell you when. Soon, I hope."

"I know, and I wish there was something I could do to make it happen right now."

A smile touches Ruby's lips.

"Maybe we need to do something big for him."

"What do you mean?"

"Something huge where he has to notice you and talk to you."

"I like where you're going with this, but what if I do something that draws attention, and he ignores me?"

"He won't."

I don't think he would either, but right now, it's a risk I'm willing to take.

Ruby and I brainstorm ideas, leaving me to decide what I should do. When she leaves, I start to clean up my desk.

That's when I find a letter from my mom.

SHAY,

I have no words to tell you how amazing The Marina looks. You put your heart into bringing it back to a place people can love and make memories. Business is good—we love that. We just don't love the idea of you putting in all the work on your own and running the business alone. The sale is happening tomorrow, and we need to do this as a family. Please be at the reality office at 3:00 p.m. as we say goodbye.

Love, Mom and Dad

THEY'RE JOKING, right?

How did they find a buyer already? I thought it wasn't going on the market till next week.

This moved much faster than I wanted.

And now they want me there.

I'm not going.

I refuse to watch my dream handed over to someone who won't cherish it the way that I do.

As for my other dream, a life with Luca?

That, I can do something about.

CHAPTER TWENTY-SEVEN

LUCA

I've never been so nervous in my entire life.

I don't know how the whole grand gesture thing works, but buying The Marina so that the woman I love and I can run it together seems like a pretty damn good place to start.

Which is how I ended up sitting in the Collins Reality office a couple of days later.

"She said she would show up?" I ask and look at Shay's parents and brother.

Her mom and dad share a look, and then her mom says, "I left her a note."

"A note?"

Her mother nods.

"Did she by chance respond to this note?"

"No, but she'll come."

"I'm not so sure she will," I admit and stand.

I glance at her dad, who smirks with a nod to the door.

I don't give anyone time to ask me where I'm going before I run out of the building and jump into my truck.

Thankfully, the roads aren't busy today, because I'm definitely speeding as I head toward Shay.

I thought it would be a cool surprise when she got to the sale and saw me. I'd confess how stubborn I was and how I'm buying The Marina so that we can run it together, but hell, I should have just gone to her and told her.

Waiting for some big moment was stupid. It's not real life. Real life is going to the woman you fell in love with the moment you knew that, through the good and the bad, you want only her at your side.

I spot her walking out of her front door the moment I pull up in front of her house.

I quickly put my truck in park and get out.

She stops dead in her tracks. "Luca," my name slips from her lips in a whisper.

"I need to talk to you," I tell her.

"Okay."

A hopeful look flashes through her eyes.

"I came to talk to you about The Marina."

Her eyes narrow and she spins back for the house.

"I don't want to talk about The Marina, Luca. If that's all you came for, you can leave."

"It's not all I came for." I follow her inside. "But it's how this starts."

"No. How this starts is, you pick up your phone or answer my texts or reply or acknowledge something I—"

"I bought The Marina!"

Her head pulls back.

"What? You … you bought it?"

I step toward her.

"Yep, that's right, Shay. I'm so far gone in love with you

that I went to your parents, who apologized, by the way, now that the truth is out, and begged them to sell me The Marina, just so I could put your name on it beside mine and we could run it together."

"You … bought The Marina?"

"Yes. Well, I'm trying to buy it, but you didn't show up today, so now here I am showing up on your doorstep so that—"

"You love me?" she asks, cutting me off mid-rant.

I pause as her tear-filled eyes gaze up at me.

Her lips twitch to smile. Of all the things I just told her, that's what she chooses to focus on?

Me.

The fact that I love her.

"You love me? After what I did?"

"I do," I say and step close enough that I can wrap my arm around her waist. I brush the other hand against her cheek, until the tips of my fingers thread through her hair. "So much, baby. I know that we won't be perfect, but you're the only person I want to be not perfect with."

She presses her lips together, and I swear to god, the fact that The Marina isn't her focus after my announcement makes my entire body relax. I'm her focus. My love for her is. And that right there is exactly why I know she's it for me. She loves that marina, but she loves me more. I'd get on my knee right now if I didn't think that was too much for her.

"Now," I begin, because even though she hasn't said she loves me, we still have papers to sign. "Are you going to get in my truck with me so we can buy this place, or are you going to stand here and argue with me?"

She answers by standing on her toes and pressing her lips to mine.

"I love you, too, Luca Asher. *So much, baby.*"

I wrap my arms around her waist and drop my head back with laughter as she smiles at me.

"I knew it."

She laughs, too, slapping my shoulder.

"Did you really buy The Marina?"

I set her to her feet.

"Do you really think I would lie about that? Your entire family is waiting there right now. Well, I think they are. I sort of left them the moment your mother said she left you a note to meet us."

But in all honesty, getting the chance to have this moment without an audience was worth it.

"You do realize this means you're tied to me legally, right?"

I grin. "Yes."

"For years."

"I do."

"You can't just decide one day that you don't want it."

"I'm aware."

"This is forever."

"I sure fucking hope so."

"Luca!" she scolds, crossing her arms and leaning into me so I can hold her tight. "I'm talking about The Marina."

"Shay, baby, if it involves you, I'm in it for life, trust me."

She's silent for a moment, but then she grabs my hand and pulls me to the door.

"Where are we going?" I ask. "The bedroom is behind us."

"Oh, trust me, as soon as we sign those papers, you'll get plenty of bedroom time with me."

"Good."

I lean in to steal another kiss, because there's no stopping me now.

"Come on. I need to show you something."

She waves for me to follow her out to her car and leads me all the way to the back and points to the driveway. There are empty soup cans tied to the back of her Jeep.

"Were you celebrating something?"

"No, I was trying to make a statement."

"And what was that?"

She opens the back door and pulls out a bright yellow sign.

I'M IN LOVE WITH LUCA ASHER is written in big bold letters with a Sharpie.

"I'm so, so sorry that I lied and I hurt you. I was scared to lose what I thought mattered the most to me, but turns out, you're that thing for me, and I was going to keep fighting until you figured it out, too. I was about to drive through town with this sign, the cans making enough noise that people had to look at me."

I know there is a huge goofy grin on my face from the way Shay rolls her eyes.

"Come here," I say and grab her hand to pull her body to mine. "I still think you should do it."

"What?" She laughs. "Really? But we just made up."

"So." I shrug. "We have to get back into town to sign those papers somehow."

Her nod is instant.

"Get in."

I race to the driver's seat, and she races to the passenger.

"I can't believe we are about to own The Marina."

I start the engine and back out of her driveway.

She squeals when we hit the road.

"Hey," I say, and she beams a smile at me.

"Yes?"

I love how happy she sounds.

I nod to the sign.

"Put that thing out the window, Shay. You owe me."

She crawls over the center to kiss me quickly then takes her seat again, rolls her window down, and sticks the sign out.

Shay Parker loves me.

I grin.

Shay Asher sounds better.

EPILOGUE

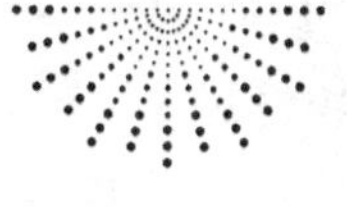

SHAY

"I'm so sorry, sir, The Marina is booked for that weekend."

I smile, even though this stranger can't see me through the phone.

Those are words I was scared I might not get to say again, but here I am, turning people away even during the winter months. Once The Marina took off, it blew us all away.

It helps that Luca got to work right away the moment he owned it, finishing the cabins and making sure we hosted event after event.

He had the idea to build an addition onto The Marina for bigger events, and from that, he added a special boardwalk to the water, which wasn't far and it's a dreamy intimate spot.

I wasn't fully into the idea, because Lovers is a small town, and having an event space takes away from the lodge. I wasn't about to step on my best friend's toes like that. But as soon as I spoke with Grace, she assured me that it'll all work out. Smaller parties are hesitant to book with them because they are so big, so having another option in our town is brilliant.

Luca and his team had it finished before the first snowfall this year, and it's been booked ever since.

"When is your next opening for the space?"

"Just after the first of the year."

"I'll take it. I'm trying to surprise my wife with a ten-year anniversary party with our closest friends and family."

"Oh, Mr. Connelly, that sounds so sweet. I've got you down and I've got your email, so I'll send you the details and payment links."

"Great."

"We'll see you in a few months," I tell him and hang up.

I immediately notice how quiet the place is. I pop out from my office and look into the dining area. There are only a few tables with guests right now, but we have a party booked for tonight, so I would imagine it will start to fill up soon.

I check my watch.

They should be here and setting up by now. Luca has been helping greet guests, so if I haven't seen him, I bet he's down there.

I say hello to each table as I cross through the dining room to the stairs that lead down to the event room's indoor entrance.

The lights are off when I reach it.

That's odd.

Luca normally has everything prepared by now. I pull my phone from my back pocket to call him, push the doors open, and flick on the lights.

My phone drops the moment the room brightens, and I suck in a breath.

It's gorgeous.

The entire space is decorated in light pink and light green. The tables are linked with cream linens and white lilies, already set with plates and utensils, ready for the night.

There is a balloon arch with a mirror in the back of the room, and the word *congratulations* over the top is the prettiest cursive I've ever seen.

I'm not sure what tonight's event is, but it's going to be amazing.

"Oh good, there you are," Carl appears from behind me. He hands me a garment bag. "I have strict orders to tell you that you have fifteen minutes to put this dress on. The guests want you here tonight."

"They want me here? At the event?"

He nods and then walks off.

"I don't even remember what event it is," I call out.

I try to recall what I saw in the books, but it just said "private event."

Still, I am the main face of this place, and if they want me here, I'll be here.

I head out the back door in the direction of my and Luca's house. He moved in with me a couple of months ago, and any outsider might think we are moving too fast, but not me. For me, we need to pick up the pace. I already know I'm going to spend my life with him. I'm ready to hit that next step.

I quickly change then pull my hair into a quick high bun before touching up my mascara. When I'm done, I unzip the dress and gasp at the long white lace dress. The detail on the sleeves is breathtaking.

It's absolutely stunning.

I run my hand over the fabric once more before slipping into it.

I feel beautiful, so I grab my phone to text Luca.

I snap a selfie and then type out *for you to remove later* before hitting send.

Then I head back to The Marina.

LUCA

I knew Shay would take longer than fifteen minutes, but just in case, everyone waited for her to leave The Marina before they piled in.

Carl, Matt, and Brian all worked swiftly to get food and drinks out for everyone, and it looks as though everyone is just as eager to get this night going as I am.

We have my family, her family, the Richfords, and all of our friends, plus a few locals here tonight. All the people I know for a fact Shay would want to share this moment with.

Is this a surprise? Yes and no.

Obviously, marrying Shay has been in my plans since the moment I knew I loved her. She knows it, I know, everyone in this town knows it.

But at this moment right here, my fingers are crossed that everything about it comes as a complete surprise to her.

Over the past six months, Shay and I have been nothing but honest and open with each other. Don't get me wrong, it has its pros, but, man, does it make it hard to surprise her.

And I want this to be the best surprise of her life.

"Are you ready for this?" Leo steps up and claps a hand to my shoulder.

I nod. "Very."

"How many weddings do you think we can squeeze into next summer?" Hudson asks with a laugh.

I don't know why his comment makes my palms sweat, but it does. I hadn't really thought about a summer wedding. Is that what Shay wants? I was just thinking of something quick and simple. I don't need the whole shebang. I just need her.

I blow out a breath.

Whatever she wants, I'll make sure she gets it.

Linc walks up and fake punches Leo in the stomach. "Well, well, if it isn't Mr. Three Pointer."

Hudson and I laugh when Leo shoves him back, his cheeks turning a slight pink.

We've been playing basketball at the local recreation center for boys' night, and we all suck tremendously, except for Leo.

He called it a "gift" one day, and the boys won't let him live it down.

A grin takes over my lips as my friends start to give each other shit about last week's game.

As soon as Shay and I bought The Marina, my friendship with Leo resumed as if it never stopped. For a moment, I thought he'd hate the idea of me being with his sister, but I think he secretly likes knowing that we're officially going to be a family someday.

Someday soon if tonight goes as planned.

"She's coming!" Grace says, speed walking through the room in my direction.

I don't hesitate as I stride past her to the front door, a couple of hoots and hollers at my back as I leave.

Shay can't come in yet. Not until I've walked her down to

the beach and dropped to my knee.

I strut out the door in my suit and misstep when I see her walking toward me.

Everything about her shines under the moonlight. It's my favorite view of Shay. Here at The Marina at night. Well, after the vision of her in bed, of course. But this Shay, this is the Shay I fell in love with. The one who makes my entire body light up when I see her. The one who is carefree and happy. The one who picked me.

"Luca Asher, what are you doing out here in a suit?" she says in a sweet voice that makes my cock jump.

Maybe I should have done this at home, alone, where I could strip her bare after.

"My presence was requested tonight."

"Mmm," she hums and leans in to kiss me.

I slide a hand around her waist to pull her to me and prolong the touch of her lips to mine. When her hand moves to my hair and threads through the strands, I slip my tongue into her mouth.

She hums again, but this time I feel it touch every part of my body.

Yep. I should have done this at home.

I pull back and groan.

"More of that later, but first, come with me."

Her eyes narrow with suspicion as she smirks.

"All right."

I lace her hand with mine and lock her in at my side as we make our way to the beach.

It's deserted, and there isn't a single thing out here that will hint at what I'm doing.

"Let's go for a dip," I say, remembering that moment over

the summer when I knew I was completely gone for this woman.

"No way," she says quickly. "It's a little chilly out here and have you seen this dress?"

"Yes, baby, I have. Which is why I suggested getting you out of it."

She leans in and kisses me.

"After this party we are oddly required to attend."

"Deal."

We both pause to look out over the water and admire the view. It's peaceful here. The water being the only surrounding sound.

"I love this lake," I say. "I fell in love with you just over there." I point to where she rushed into the water that night.

"You're so cheesy." She leans her head on my shoulder. "And I love it."

"And right there"—I twist to point at The Marina, the glow of the dining room we spent countless hours remodeling after dark shines back at us—"was where I knew that I'd met the woman of my dreams."

Shay is looking up at me, her eyes are glistening as she bites her bottom lip.

"And right here, this is the spot where I ask you to be my wife."

I slowly lower to one knee, and Shay gasps.

"Luca! Are you serious?"

I nod and smile.

"I've never been more serious. I love you with all my heart, Shay Parker, and I know I'm not perfect and I say cheesy lines and I can be a little dramatic at times, but I also know that I will spend every day I breathe making you feel loved, cherished, and valued while supporting every dream of yours for as long as you let me. I get only one life, and I want it with you. Will you marry me?"

"Yes!" she screams and leans quickly to kiss me, but I pull back just as fast.

"I forgot to pull out the ring," I say and reach into my pocket. "I was so eager to ask you to be my wife, I spaced it."

I pop the box open, revealing an oval solitaire diamond with a simple white gold band to Shay. Then I slip it onto her finger.

"Your wife," she says, smiling at the ring and then at me. "I love the sound of that."

She pulls me in for another kiss, reaching for my belt.

"Let's swim now," she says, her eyes dancing with suggestion.

I groan loudly and lean back.

"We can't … yet."

"Why not?"

I rub the back of my neck.

I really should have done this alone.

"We sort of have a party to attend."

"I don't even know whose party it is," Shay says, now reaching for the bottom of her dress.

It pains me, but I place my hand on hers to stop her from undressing.

"It's our party."

"What?" She freezes.

"Come on." I grab her hand and tug her back to the new building. "Everyone is waiting for the future Mr. and Mrs. Asher to join them."

She squeals and then takes off at a run, pulling me with her.

She bursts through the door and holds up her left hand. "Luca Asher is off the market!"

Then she leans into me, kissing me once more before our friends and family swarm us for hugs.

Our eyes lock over her mother's shoulder, and the biggest smile touches her lips.

Then she mouths *my office, five minutes.*

I grin and nod, knowing it'll be nearly impossible to sneak away right now.

But when it comes to Shay, whatever she wants, it's hers.

Want more from Luca and Shay?
Keep reading for an exclusive bonus scene.

BONUS EPILOGUE

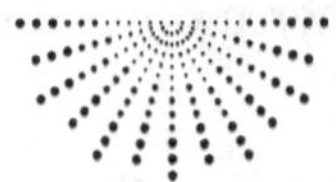

LUCA - FOUR YEARS LATER

"Yes!" I scream, my throat starting to hurt from my excitement.

The little hand in mine flinches and then softly touches my arm.

"Daddy, why are you being so noisy?" I glance down at my four-year-old daughter, Rose, and grin.

"I'm cheering on Uncle Huddy and his team."

"You're loud."

Shay chuckles on the other side of Rose. I glance at my wife and then at her hand, where it's smoothing up and down over her belly.

The Asher clan is growing fast. Ruby might have started it with Max, but Shay and I kept it going with Rose and Ryan, who is sitting on Leo's lap next to Shay.

Slow and steady has never really been our thing, and Shay getting pregnant just weeks after we got engaged made sense. Then, after two years and a wedding, she was pregnant again and now … again. Having one girl and one boy, we made the choice not to know the sex in advance for this one, but I'm keeping my fingers crossed for a girl.

The crowd screams more as Hudson's hockey team scores another goal. They've been on fire this season, and today is no different.

The clock ticks down, and the buzzer rings through the arena.

Hudson's team won.

"Okay, troops, let's move," I say, grabbing Rose to carry her out so I don't lose her in the crowd.

"Can I ride on your shoulders, daddy?" she asks, and I don't hesitate. Up she goes.

Behind me, a nice drool bubble slides down Ryan's chin, and Leo rolls his eyes.

"Ryan, my man, we keep the spit in our mouth."

Shay laughs, waddling behind me. I wait for her just past the door to the eating area where heat swarms us. I sling an arm around her shoulders and kiss the top of her head.

Leo's girls run in front of us, and one calls out for Rose, so I put her down. She runs to follow her cousins as I walk toward my dad, Miles, Quinn, and Sadie, all standing by the trophy case.

It's wild to think that this is my life now. I've always been the sappier one in the family, but heck, I can't imagine a better life than the one I have.

My phone buzzes with a text from Carl.

He has recently been promoted to general manager of The Marina. We've been booked out more than three months for the last two years, and with business doing so well, Shay was able to hire more and step back to help with the kids. It was her choice, of course. I do my best, but damn, moms are like superheroes, and they don't get enough credit.

I can hand Ryan a cup of Cheerios, and he'll toss it back in my face. Shay will pick up every piece of cereal, put it back in the cup, hand it to him, and he'll say, "Mommy, I love you."

I can't blame the kid.

She's the best person we know.

Speaking of Shay, she appears at my side with Ryan on her hip and Rose by her side.

She grins up at me, and I take that moment to pull her into me and press my lips to hers softly. I feel her entire body relax at my touch, and even after all these years together, knowing that I'm the one who can make her feel that way sends a spark through my body. I tilt her chin and press my lips to hers.

Miles clears his throat. "There are children present."

"It was a simple peck." I laugh.

"Mm-hmm." He glances at each of my children and then at Shay's belly. "That's how it starts."

"Are you still planning to host breakfast in the morning?" Sadie asks.

"We wouldn't miss it," Shay answers, and the two of them quickly start planning who is bringing what. More people means more food, but we never miss a Sunday. Shay's parents come from time to time, and even though my Dad has never admitted it, I know he loves having them around more and more.

"Don't skimp on the bacon this time," Hudson says, finally making his appearance of the night.

"Great game," I say, and he pulls me in for a side hug.

"I'm glad you could all come." He makes a silly face at Rose and then flicks one of her pigtails.

"Uncle Huddy, are you going to put me on your team someday?"

"You bet. Just let me know when you're ready."

"I'm ready!"

"Good. That's a lot more excitement than your dad used to have."

I roll my eyes just as Shay places her hand on my chest. I glance down in time to see Ryan close his eyes and rest his head on her shoulder. "I think it's time to head home."

I nod, and we all quickly exchange hugs and well wishes for safe driving.

Then I pick up my daughter, take Shay's hand in mine, and start for the car.

To go home.

With my kids and *my wife*.

Please consider visiting Amazon to leave a review

What happens when you move back to your hometown, move in next door to your enemy, but soon find yourself inviting him to move in with you?

Find out in Ruby and Declan's book, Holding You!

MORE BOOKS BY JAMI ROGERS

THE ASHER FAMILY

(A Small Town Series)

Promise Me

An Enemies to Lovers Romance

Loving You

A Fake Dating Romance

Tempting Me

An Enemies to Lovers Romance

Holding You

An Enemies to Lovers Romance

THE WIND VALLEY SERIES

(A Small Town Series)

The Write One

An Enemies to Lovers Romance

Write About You

A Fake Dating Romance

The Write Choice

An Enemies to Lovers / Best Friend's Sister Romance

Write That Down

A Runaway Bride / Opposites Attract Romance

More Than Write

A Single Dad Grump Sunshine Romance

Always Been Write

A Friends to Lovers Romance

THE KISS ME SERIES

(A Small Town New Adult Series)

Kiss Me Crazy

An Enemies to Lovers Romance

Love is Crazy

A Friends to Lovers Romance

I Want Crazy

An Unplanned Baby Romance

THE EVERGREEN BROTHERS SERIES

(A Small Town Series)

A Boyfriend by Christmas

An Enemies to Lovers Romance

The Summer Wedding Hoax

A Friends to Lovers Romance

A Match by Christmas

An Enemies to Lovers Romance

THE BLACK ALCOVE SERIES

(A Small Town New Adult Series)

Just One Kiss

An Enemies to Lovers Romance

Just One Night

A Friends to Lovers Romance

Just One Touch

A Single Dad / Best Friend's Sister Romance

Just One Moment

An Enemies to Lovers Romance

Just One Spark

An Office Romance

Just One Love

A Friends to Lovers / Fake Dating Romance

Standalone Novels

Love Money

An Undercover Cop Romance

FOLLOW JAMI

Want more from Jami?

Join Jami's mailing list for exclusive bonus epilogues,
giveaways, and all the book news!

Visit her website
www.authorjamirogers.com

Or join her (very new) Facebook group
Jami Rogers Readers

facebook.com/AuthorJamiRogers

instagram.com/authorjamirogers

bookbub.com/authors/authorjamirogers

goodreads.com/jamirogers

tiktok.com/@authorjamirogers

ACKNOWLEDGMENTS

This series has been so much fun to write, and I am so thankful that readers are loving it. So THANK YOU for reading my books and falling for my characters as much as I have. You are the best part of this journey!

Thank you, as always, to HangLe, Julie, Dana, Emma, and Erika for making this book so truly amazing! I would not be here without you.

Cheers to the next book!

ABOUT THE AUTHOR

My name is Jami Rogers and I write fun, fast, and flirty slow-burn contemporary romance novels with heat. I *love* love and want to share my passion for happily ever afters with the world.

I was born in Wyoming and still live in the cowboy state with my husband, daughter, and dog. I like to read, write, run, watch movies/TV, and spend time with my family. I'm horrible at returning phone calls and prefer to text, but I still struggle to hit the little blue arrow to send a message once I'm finished typing my reply. My husband does 90% of the cooking in our house. Not because I'm busy – I'm just simply a lousy cook.

www.authorjamirogers.com

Want more from Jami?
Join Jami's mailing list for exclusive bonus epilogues, giveaways, and all the book news!

facebook.com/AuthorJamiRogers

instagram.com/authorjamirogers

goodreads.com/jamirogers

bookbub.com/profile/jami-rogers

tiktok.com/@authorjamirogers

www.ingramcontent.com/pod-product-compliance
Lightning Source LLC
Chambersburg PA
CBHW021037310726
48969CB00006B/1693